FREEWILL

CHRIS LYNCH

FREEWILL

HARPERCOLLINS*PUBLISHERS*

Library of Congress Cataloging-in-Publication Data

Lynch, Chris.

Freewill / Chris Lynch.

p.   cm.

Summary: A teenager trying to recover from the tragic death of his father and stepmother believes himself to be responsible for the rash of teen suicides occurring in his town.

ISBN 0-06-028176-6 — ISBN 0-06-028177-4

[1. Emotional problems—Fiction.   2. Death—Fiction.   3. Grandparents—Fiction.]   I. Title.

PZ7.L979739 Fr   2001

[Fic]—dc21   00-032050

Book design by Alison Donalty

1 3 5 7 9 10 8 6 4 2

First Edition

FOR JULIANNE

FREEWILL

FAITH

"NICE TABLE."

"What?"

"I said, nice table, that. Pretty work. The inlay is classic. And it's strong, huh?"

He stands on the table, adding eighteen inches to his height. He bounces up and down on his toes, testing the table's strength and adding, taking away, adding and taking away, an additional two inches. He hops down, to where nature put him. Five foot seven. Do you know this one's name? No, you don't. Don't and won't.

"But it doesn't look it. That's what's really nice about work like this. Real strong and functional, but with delicate lines. Nice, nice work."

He is sliding his hand over the highly polished finish of the nice, nice work in question.

"Thanks. But it's not mine," you say.

"What? What are you talking about? Of course it's yours."

"No. Sorry, but it isn't."

"Yes, it is. What are you, jerking me around? I been

sitting here three feet away from you for two weeks watching you do it."

Watching you. Watching you? Two weeks watching *you*.

"You just finished it yesterday morning. It's just dry
today. It's nice work, why you want to pretend you didn't
do it?"

You look at that table, and you agree. It is nice work.

"Two weeks?" you ask. "Does it really take somebody
two weeks of life to make something like that?"

"Fine. Be that way."

The surface of the table is the size of a chessboard.
Your classmate has left it to get back to his own knotty-
pine creation which he says is a bookshelf, but you know
is for videos.

Why are you here?

Whose table is that?

Why are you in wood shop? You are meant to be a
pilot. How does wood shop get you any closer to being a
pilot?

But here you are. And you do not like to be idle.
Devil's workshop and all. You don't know why you are
here but you know you are, and you are meant to be doing
something so you might as well.

Why would somebody spend two weeks of his life on
a table big enough for one small lamp, one can of Pringles
and one glass of water and nothing else?

And why would another somebody spend two weeks
watching him?

Beautiful plank of blond oak. Four feet long, two feet wide, two inches deep. Little table maybe means nothing, but this is a beautiful piece of wood.

"This is a beautiful piece of wood, Mr. Jacks. May I?"

"Yes it is, and yes you may, and what's more I have fifteen others just like it stacked up in the storage. Sweetheart deal, fell from the sky, and you shoppers are the beneficiaries."

You stroke the piece of wood as if it were an Angora cat. You could do that stroke up or down or sideways or swirls all day long if you wanted to and never pick up a splinter. It is a magnificent piece of wood.

"That mean you're finished with that table now?"

"'Scuse?"

"The table. You filing it?"

Your classmate takes this as his cue, sliding on over beside you. "He says it ain't his, Mr. Jacks."

"Well it's not, if he's finished with it. It's the school's. Just like that video rack is going to be if you ever complete it."

"It's a bookshelf, sir."

"Right."

"You done with the table then?" Mr. Jacks, just like the video-shelving guy, takes an up-close-and-personal inspection of the table in question. "Nice finish. I can see myself. Extra credit when I can see myself. Smooth, strong, clean edges. Fine work, as usual."

The kid is laughing in a way that makes clear to everybody that he doesn't find anything funny. "He says it's not his, sir."

"It's not mine."

"No, sorry to say," Mr. Jacks says, "but it isn't. I wish I could let you guys keep some of your stuff, but the rules are the rules. We keep them through term, then we donate."

Mr. Jacks takes the table up and walks it off, to where they take the wood that has been made furniture and is thus no longer of any use to the class.

"Mr. Jacks." You are looking ever closer at that beautiful blond board and all its fine grains.

"Huh? Oh, ya, knock yourself out. But it better be great, using my star lumber."

"Great," you say. An answer. "Great," you repeat, a question, a promise, a further question.

Why do you do it? What is the driver? You don't know.

"What are you making there, Will?" Mr. Jacks asks.

You release the trigger on the handsaw, raise your protective glasses. "Not sure, really." The rest of the class continues with hammering, planing, chipping and slicing with pneumatic tools and raw muscle power, so that you have to strain to be heard. But this is not new. It is standard and barely noticeable, to have to strain to be heard.

"Well, it's rather important that you know what you're making. Otherwise, how can I judge whether you've made it or not when you're done?"

4

You look up, and try to smile. You do smile, successfully if not radiantly. "Faith, Mr. Jacks," is what you say.

"Faith," he says. "Faith. You mean I'm just supposed to trust you, that you're doing something worthwhile with your time and my wood and the school's machinery?"

"Well. Well, I suppose that's what I'm saying, sir."

Mr. Jacks looks all around, for comic effect, the way teachers do in regular classrooms when they want to emphasize that a student has said something fairly ridiculous. But this is not the regular class, nobody hears or notices what is going on between you two, and Mr. Jacks has to give an answer all on his own.

"Okay," he says. "You haven't botched anything so far. So I guess you've earned a little faith."

Is it? Is it faith if you've earned it? Isn't faith putting trust in something for no good reason? Maybe you should ask.

Or maybe you shouldn't. Since you have no idea what it is you're doing, or why.

This means you.

Asking you. Is there a voice in your head, directing you what to do? Is that how it gets done, what gets done?

If so, why do you listen? Is it authority because it is in your head? Or is it in your head because it is authority?

"Gran? Hello? Pops?"

Nobody is home. This is not all that unusual, they are largely functional people still, and do go out from time to time. But they were supposed to be home this afternoon. That's how it was supposed to be, and you really prefer things to be the way they are supposed to be.

Funny, when you find things to be not to your liking you try to force them to be otherwise.

"Gran?" you call again, louder. "Pops." The house is small. It is easy enough to know when no one is in it, and yelling louder doesn't conjure them. Neither does standing frozen in the doorway.

Go on. Step inside. There's no other way. There will be a reasonable explanation. Check the refrigerator. The refrigerator. There wouldn't be a note anyplace else, and you know that. The grandparents are not thumbtack people, they are magnet people. You know that. And do you see any metal walls around here? Go on, go to the fridge.

Will. Went to bocce ball. Beautiful day. Come on down. Love, Gran & Pops.

And here's the thing. You do it once more, don't you. Like the note is lying to you or something. Like there is some kind of conspiracy.

"Gran?" you call. "Pops?"

She is so right. It is a magnificent day. You stare up searching for a cloud and see but one anemic-looking excuse for a wisp of a nothing probably a thousand miles away in the sky. The rest of what you take in is such a deep and hard crystalline blue, like a swimming pool, that you feel drenched in it after staring up for only one minute. One minute is a great deal of sky-staring for most people. It is nothing to you. The clack of bocce balls against one another plays as the soundtrack.

"So how was it today?" Gran says, first grabbing, then pulling on your arm as if you were a window shade and she wanted you down.

"Sorry, Gran?"

"Shush," Pops says. He is lined up, staring down the improbably perfect crew cut of the bowling green. His size-twelve feet are tight together, his elbows bent, the ball resting just under his chin. He is stooped over as he addresses the ball, but truth be told he would be stooped over anyway. Pops is a stooped-over man.

"It was good today, Gran."

"Shush, I said. Did you hear me say shush? This is a critical shot."

He shushes you a lot, doesn't he? Does he like you, do you suppose? Or does he tolerate you? Those are the choices anyway, right? Like or tolerate? Love wouldn't come into it, would it? No, you don't suppose love would . . .

"Started on a gorgeous piece of wood today, Gran. Even without doing anything to it, it's a thing of beauty. It's too good to be furniture. It should be growing in your garden, but of course, it can't. So I'm going to set it free."

Pops drops his ball right there on the perfect green ground. Slowly he turns to face the two of you, wife and grandson, sum total of family. "Did you even hear me, Will?" He gestures toward the little cluster of black balls down at the other end of the pitch. Like, if you see them, you will comprehend. "I told you what a critical shot this was, and you know I can't bowl properly if you two are conversing."

Do you like him, Will? Or do you just tolerate him? Or does it even matter? Don't suppose it does. You're essentially . . . what would they call it . . . a *circumstance*, until—god willing, as they say—you turn eighteen at least.

"Are you listening to me, Will?"

"Oh Pops, take your shot, after all." Gran calls Pops Pops. You like that, don't you. And she doesn't take him always so seriously. You like that, too. She does manage to be very kind, doesn't she?

They are kind to you. Kind people. Kindly. They didn't have to take you in. Or did they? Love? Is it love? Charity. Somewhere in the Bible, doesn't it indicate that they are both the same thing? Does that matter to you either way?

Pops bowls, finally, after taking a good long time lining himself up again. Twice as long as he needed, that's for sure, but he had to be dramatic about how you had inconvenienced him, and then he must have put a mighty backspin on the thing because it took about a month to reach its destination where it nestled snugly among its colleagues.

"Pretty shot, Pops," you say.

Pops is pleased. He is rubbing his hands eagerly as he walks back to you. "Ya, wasn't bad, huh? You playing today, Mister?"

You look up, at the sky, down, at the almost grainless surface of the lawn, left, at the creamy well-kept skin of Gran's face under her sensible massive sun hat, and finally right, at the bronze road map of Pops's gnarly mug.

"Sure, I'm playing," you say.

"Good," Pops says, clapping his hands loudly and rubbing them together hard enough to light a fire. "I'm gonna kick your ass, boy."

He always says that, doesn't he? Funny. But wouldn't you really like to know how much of it is play and how much of it is spastic honesty?

"Ya Pops," you say. "You are going to kick my ass, I know it."

That's what you always say, too. Is that what you want to say? Wouldn't you like to say something else? How would it feel?

Better? Might you feel . . . *better*? Would you like that?

"Hmm," she says thoughtfully.

"Hello?"

Angela is standing over you. You are sitting. If you were standing, she would still be standing over you. She is tall, hard in a track-star way because she is a track star, and has a closely cut orange Afro probably an inch thick all around. Has she spoken to you before? You know her name, though, don't you. Haven't bothered knowing any of the others. What's the use, after all. But you haven't been able to not know Angela.

"You're Angela, right?"

"Right." She is talking to the woodwork. "Hmm."

"Hmm."

"So what does it do?"

"Do?"

"Do."

"This?"

"This."

"Um. Doesn't do anything, far as I know."

"So what's it gonna be then, when it's finished?"

You are both staring at it now, as if it were one of those alien patterns in a wheat field, or a crying Virgin Mary statue.

"It already is what it's going to be."

"Which is?"

We all wait.

"I don't know."

"Oh come on. What does it *mean*?"

What does it mean? Do you think it means something? Does it have to mean something?

"Everything means something."

"Oh. Okay. Well maybe that's true. And maybe this means something. But if it does, then I don't know what."

"You might not know what. But I bet you there is an answer."

"So why are you making a pole?"

"Shut up. It's not a pole, it's a coat tree. Just doesn't have any branches yet."

"Sorry."

Angela is leaving. Back to work. Done with you.

"I like your hair."

She stops, does a half turn. "Thanks. Didn't do it for you, however."

"I liked it better when it was yellow, though."

"Well I think I'll keep it like this just the same."

"Do you know what today is? May fourteenth? It's one year ago today Sinatra died."

She waits for you to make any sense at all. She'll be waiting a long time for that, won't she.

"Sorry about that, but I'm still sticking with orange."

"How do you figure, a guy as rotten as him, could do something as moving as 'Summer Wind'? Is there any sense in that, do you think?"

Is there any sense?

Angela shrugs.

She goes back to honing an already well-honed trunk of a limbless coat tree.

She is back.

"So why does it look like a penis then, huh? Why you sitting over here quiet like a monk, working on a big ol' penis all this time, huh?"

Angela is a tad piqued. Not unpleasant. But piqued still.

You look seriously, closely, at your work.

"Does it, you think? Look like that? I don't really think it does. Does it though?"

"Yes."

"So that's why you were talking to me?" You look at your thing. "Because I offended you?"

"Yes."

"Well I don't think that's what I'm making. No, now that I look at it, I really don't think that's what I'm making."

Funny, how Angela looks at you, *at* you, the same way she looks at the piece. You are a study.

"Fine. Maybe it isn't."

You are looking at each other now a very long time. Nothing much comes of it, though.

She walks.

"See ya."

"Mr. Jacks. Mr. Jacks, I'm done here. Would it be possible to start on another one of those nice pieces of board in your stash?"

"You're *done*? With *that*?" Mr. Jacks is marching over now, with a sense of purpose. He's staring burn holes in the wood and you know what he wants.

He wants *what*. And he wants *why*.

But you can't give them to him.

It's not as if you invented it, whatever it is, anyhow, is it? Does anyone else know what they're doing? Or why? Do you think that stops anybody from doing what they do?

Take a look at what people do, Will. Go ahead. Look. See if any of it makes any sense. He can't make you do what nobody can do. He can't make you explain.

Jacks is standing over you now. You and yours. Lips pursed, finger pointing.

But then he goes limp. As if he has played the scene out in his head, he has seen where it does and doesn't go. And is drained by the effort. He knows why you are both here. He knows both your limits.

"Go ahead, take another board," he says.

Why is it you should do the shopping? Not that you mind doing the shopping, you don't, at all. It's the *why* that nags. That is, it's *their* shopping. Do you have some kind of cosmic debt because you have been stuck with them? Isn't that, isn't this, life? You are theirs, are you not? Theirs? *You* didn't kill anybody. Did you? Did you, Will, kill anybody?

Of course not. So why do you owe them? Why should it be that you are treated like an imposition? What does it mean? That you don't belong? That you don't belong there? That you don't belong to them? That's a shame. That's a dirty damn shame. Tough break, kid.

"Hello," Angela says. She is half-buried in a survey of the comparative unit prices of Green Giant and store-brand garden peas. She waves a can, then gets back to business.

"Hello," you say, a little startled. You continue on.

13

Next aisle, breakfast cereals.

"Hello," you say, as if you have not already said it.

Angela is walking with her mother and a bulging cart. Mother looks much like daughter, and not all that much older, either. Good skin. Not as tall and muscular. Softer. Walking into a dance, you might very well make a run for the mom.

"Hello," Angela says, grinning like people do at nuts.

Next aisle, pastas, rices, sauces and whatnot. No mother. Angela.

You burble at her. "I just never figured, I guess, you to be doing the shopping-type stuff, y'know."

"And I never figured you, to be eating, y'know, food-type stuff."

Angela laughs first at her own joke, which gives you the green light to laugh too. She's peeking now, and poking at your cart while you look all over nervously, as if she is poking around your underwear rather than your produce.

"What is with all this creamed corn, All-Bran, prunes . . ."

"My grandparents. I shop, for them." You pull your cart back away from Angela slightly, protectively.

She gets the message. "Sorry," she says. Sounds insulted. "Didn't mean to go there. Just making conversation."

You edge your cart back toward hers, offering another peek. Clumsy. Bump.

She smiles. "Thanks, anyway, but I've had enough thrills for today. See ya."

"See ya."

And she is gone and you are standing, like a cardboard whatever parked in front of an unmanned display selling old-folks groceries. You sneak a look over your shoulder, catch her rounding the corner, and snap into gear.

She has skipped the next aisle, but you are ten feet of the way up before realizing, so you continue on, make the turn, and start a slow-motion pursuit through cosmetics and toothpaste and deodorant.

What will you do though? You don't, do you? You don't *do*, do you? Do you even know why you are following her?

You slow down. Slow down some more. Angela's mother rounds the corner, looks at you, and you know the look. The I've-seen-you-and-now-I'm-seeing-you-again-too-soon-and-what-do-you-want-with-us look. Fact of life, you make people nervous. You see it, and you wince. Angela, apparently, sees it too. Looks at her mother, follows her line of vision, traces it back to you.

"Hey," she says. "You following me? Or are you lost?"

And you don't even have an answer for that soft line, do you?

"Sorry," you say, and busy yourself pawing through the medicated shampoos for old flaking scalps.

You can't see, because you are intensely trying not to

see, but you can hear, somewhat. Angela's mother is nervously asking what on earth you are. Angela is, in fits and stops, trying to tell her.

Might be nice to hear, what you are.

Might not.

"What are you doing?"

"Sorry, Angela. Sorry."

"Do stop apologizing. Just, like, what are you doing? Are you okay? 'Cause, you don't seem it, you know. And you are scaring my mother."

"Oh. Damn. Should I speak to her?"

"Ah, no. Thanks anyway. But are you following me for a reason?"

"I'm not—"

"I don't date guys, just for the record."

"Just for the record, neither do I—I mean, that's not, I'm not like that . . . I don't date, like, anybody, so you don't have to worry."

"Didn't say I was worried."

No, she doesn't look worried. You don't worry her. That's good. More than good, that's *it*. Can you think of anyone else you don't worry?

"I should finish the shopping," you say.

"Ya, so should I. Don't you hate it?"

You'd like to say you do. Just to be agreeing with her. And to approximate the normal behavior of a seventeen-year-old guy.

"I kind of like it, really." You shrug. Perfect for you,

16

you know. The shrug. Even if it isn't what you mean. What do you mean, Will?

"See, this is what I mean," Mr. Jacks says as the two of you leaf through the photo album. "Where did all this go?"

You have no idea where it went, or where it came from in the first place.

"I don't know what to tell you, Mr. Jacks."

"You recognize it, though, right? I mean, that desk there," he points, madly flips pages, "that corner cabinet," flip, flip, flip, "and of course these . . ."

These are the worst of it. *These* are so grotesque you cannot believe it.

"What are you laughing at, Will? They are beautiful. You have every reason to be proud of work like that."

Every reason. Except one. You don't have the primary reason to be proud of work like that. You don't remember *doing* work like that.

"Yes, Mr. Jacks. Sorry."

But you cannot stop staring at page after page of this garish nightmare that you are supposed to be so proud of. Angela wants to talk about penises? She should have a look at this gallery of freakish penile gnomes so carefully sculpted and hand-painted in loving detail down to the laugh lines spiking out of their charming soulless eyes. And whirligigs, with their fantastical shapes, improbable forms, and propellers to nowhere. Scores of them, all the work of an exceptional craftsman who must have worked hundreds of hours on them.

Who was you.

Why?

All those hours. All that concentration. All that dedication to craft.

Why?

"Why?" you blurt.

Good boy. For once. That's the stuff. If you're going to listen to voices, why not listen to your own?

Alas, Mr. Jacks doesn't get it. Doesn't get why you asked why. Doesn't get the important part anyway. The important part is the complicated part. Is the hard, hard part. It's not Mr. Jacks's job, to get that part.

"Why," he repeats calmly, "is that, I think it is better for you to keep that kind of variety in your work, rather than what you are now doing. You will advance much further in woodworking by broadening your—"

"I'm supposed to be a pilot, Mr. Jacks. How did I wind up in wood shop? What good does wood shop do for a pilot?"

That is the stuff. Why indeed. Go on, go get it.

Mr. Jacks takes a good long sigh. That is never good, is it? He leans far back in his squeaky wooden chair, behind his well-turned hard pine desk, looking like one of the important administrators of the school except for the smell and faint dusting of wood powder that is settled on everything in the office including Mr. Jacks himself.

"I am sorry, Will, for what happened to your folks. I am truly sorry, for what has been dealt you. But we have to move ahead . . ."

Do you like that *we*, Will?

". . . The requirements, for your program, can't be any different than . . . somebody else's. In fact, it's even more important now, that I don't let you slip through the cracks. You are not a pilot, and never were. The aptitude tests don't lie, okay? And the tests indicated that . . . you don't have the skill set, for a pilot. As I understand it, Will, you don't even drive, is that correct? Most guys your age can't *wait—*"

"Surfaces," you say, stopping him dead. "Surfaces . . . are what I don't like. Doesn't mean I couldn't operate a car or a boat or a motorcycle if I wanted to. I just . . . see myself flying *above* stuff, you know, Mr. Jacks? That's what I'd be better at. That's all."

That's all. Is that all? You expect he'll hand you your wings now?

He nods. He is good at nodding. From practice, and from wanting to nod, agree, understand. Even if he doesn't.

"The assessment said you would be good with this kind of work, Will. And you are."

You wait. Wait for what, Will? He said his bit. That's his bit. Do you want to say yours? Do you think he's right? Do you think anything is right?

"I'm a pilot, Mr. Jacks, not a woodworker."

Jacks gets frustrated, bangs his index finger hard

off one photo after another. "You used to be a wood-worker. Used to be an excellent woodworker. Do you mind telling me just exactly what it is you're doing out there now?"

He is pointing toward the door that leads from his office to the classroom/shop, where all the other students are most likely inching closer to get a listen. You should run over and throw the door open to catch them, Will. Would you like to do that?

"I don't know."

He sighs again. "Will, there are four of them already. You gotta know what they are."

You shake your head. It is a strong move, your head shake. The only strong move in your bag, wouldn't you say?

"Honestly, Mr. Jacks. I don't."

He stands up. Walks around his desk, over to the wall where pictures of the finest works of wood from the cream of his students of the last ten years are represented in carefully arranged photographs. He looks like he's shopping for something that he has misplaced, but as everyone knows he spends hours on end going over that wall. You know he is merely stalling. He doesn't know what to do with you. It's not the woodman's job, to know what to do with you.

Nobody knows what to do with you.

"Will you do something for me, Will? I'd like you to make me a nice gnome. Would you make me a nice gnome? I showed some of your stuff to my mom, right, who has this big garden, and she said she would really like to have one of those nice gnomes you do, only sort of customized for her with an extra-big chubby, happy face. Then maybe a whirligig if that works out. I know we're bending the rules a bit but it's a technicality because as a local senior she would be eligible at the end of the term to select the piece anyway. And I do want to see your stuff get publicized. You are very gifted, you know, Will, and if word started circulating, who knows what this could do for you. So." He puts his hand on your back, eases you up out of the chair and toward the door as if the two of you have agreed to the deal—or he has just fired you—and sees you out.

A nice gnome. A *nice* gnome.

Angela slides over your way once you are settled back at your post, sizing up a block of wood, and staring.

"That was a long meeting. What did you do to deserve that?"

"A nice gnome," you say.

"Come again?"

"He wants me to make a nice gnome for his mom."

"Ooooh. You mean those nasty little horrors you used to make all the time before you started making these what-the-hells over here?"

There would be no shame in getting irritated with all this by now. No shame, Will.

"Ya," you say solemnly. "He wants one of those."

She laughs. "Guess his mother did some terrible shit when he was little, huh?"

The radio is playing. Are you listening? Listen. No, *listen.* Down at the pond, last night. Somebody was killed. Listen, Will. You didn't know her. She was your age. You sort of knew her. She didn't go to your school. Are you listening? You have to be waking up anyhow. Somebody was killed. A pretty girl who went to school not far from here. You knew her, though not real well. She was very nice. She drowned. Very mysterious. Cops don't know what is going on. Won't know until they investigate. You're awake now. Sad, no? These things are so sad. Aren't they so sad?

And they just never, never, stop. They keep coming at you.

But you do keep setting the alarm to wake you up to it.

You knew her, didn't you?

"Maybe you want to stay home today," Gran says as she wastes another valuable minute of her diminishing time on this earth whipping up some oatmeal and whipping it down in front of you. "I don't see the harm. Pops, do you see the harm, if he takes a day off today?"

"I don't see the harm," Pops says. He probably doesn't see the harm. He sees the newspaper pretty well though.

"So there, see, it is a good idea. Beautiful day like this,

a young man like yourself in the prime of life. You should be able to take a day now and again. Your grandfather and I will be going to the bowling green, and you could too. Then we'll take you to lunch. What do you think, Pops?"

Pops looks up from the paper, and you can see he's been frozen in a grimace. "Ya," he says. "Ya, we could do that."

You take four or five decent-sized spoonfuls of oat-meal, which is more than usual and not at all easy for you to manage. To be polite. And reassuring. Then you stand to go.

"I'm fine, Gran," you say, standing directly in front of her. The two of you stand there, like the two of you do. Not kissing or hugging or patting shoulders or shaking hands. Not contacting.

Gran wakes up to the same news you do. She knows.

Why does she worry so much? What does she think you're going to do?

"Really, I'm fine. I have stuff I have to do at shop. I'll check the green on the way home and if you guys are there I'll come play. Okay?"

She just looks at you, little lined corners of her mouth turned down like that. "Okay," she finally says, though she seems to want to go with you to school rather than go bowling in the sun.

"How's it coming?" Mr. Jacks asks brightly.

How's it coming. It's a block of soft wood with a few

chips lopped off it. It's nothing yet. He knows it, you know it, his mother knows it. Tell him that.

You stare at it. "Coming along, Mr. Jacks. Taking shape." You are looking at it as if it is staring back.

Is there a face in there, Will?

It is an ungodly massive and professional-caliber high school stadium, representing the other half of the school's occupational-therapy approach to education. "Busy hands and busy feet, keeps the sad sacks off the street." It's not on a plaque anywhere. You all just sort of know it.

You sit up in the stands, a soft air rubbing up and over your face. You eat a bag of cheese curls and watch her every move even though from this vantage point in the highest reaches of the stands it is hard to follow any one being. From here it looks like an army of busy, possessed little creatures—ants stocking their nest, or slave peoples building pyramids. Everywhere, athletes are doing their thing—sprinting, jogging, stretching, throwing. You think there will be accidents eventually, pile-ups like on the expressway, but nobody seems to cross anybody else out, even if they all cross paths.

And Angela does it all. She must be one of those Greek things—decca, hepta—some kind of 'thlete, because she no sooner finishes spiking that javelin than she is out on the oval track, orange head bobbing around four hundred meters like the taillights on a springy jacked-up old Camaro.

When she cruises to a stop, she tails off the track at the foot of your section of bleachers. She walks in a way you only ever see track speedsters and campy flamey guys do, all loose floppy legs thrown way out ahead of them and hands placed flat over their own kidneys as if giving themselves spontaneous back rubs.

She looks up, right at you.

So what? What are you doing? What's so wrong about that? There are more athletes on the ground than there are watchers in the seats because who is really interested in watching high school runners do their boring meaningless training stuff on a brilliant afternoon? You can be seen, up there in your perch, like they cannot. So what? Are you doing something wrong? If you were, would you know?

You look down, concentrate hard on your cheese curls. Two left. One left. Crumbs. Tip the bag up. Drink the last of the cheese powder, whey powder, salt, color, monosodium glutamate all down. Wipe the orange bits off your lip.

You look down again. She's moving on. You have survived it, whatever it was. Though look there, she is glancing back over her shoulder. Like she doesn't have anything better to do than worry about you.

Up you get, and down you go, back out of the stadium. You have things to do anyway, rather than spend your valuable hours watching some sport that hardly anybody cares about even when it is a competition, never mind practice.

• • •

Did you hear that? They have not ruled out suicide. They have not ruled it out. But of course they haven't. They never do, do they? Are you listening? If you didn't want to get up you wouldn't have set the clock radio for six forty-five on the all-news-all-the-time station. So listen. Are you listening? They have not ruled out suicide. She may have done it herself, but they are not sure.

How screwed is that, that they can't be sure? Of course they can't be sure. They can *never, ever* be sure, and they are lying sacks of dirt to ever claim that they can. Isn't that right?

Suicide is still a possibility, says mister investigator. You could have told him that.

Because you know what he knows what we all know. That as an alternative to absolutely everything, suicide can never be ruled out.

That's why we have it.

Neither can foul play, adds mister investigator. He'll keep you posted. On the bright side, a lovely memorial to the girl is accumulating at the site. Flowers. Cards. Notes. Bears, and things. People care. People are good.

"Okay, so are you following me for real? Am I supposed to think now it was a coincidence that you found me at the supermarket? What gives with you?"

"Nothing. I just wanted to watch track-and-field practice, that's all."

"Nobody watches practice. Practically nobody watches *meets*. What are you after?"

"I'm not after anything."

"I told you I don't date guys. I did tell you that, right?"

"You did. I'm not looking for a date."

"So then what *are* you looking for? And what could you possibly want from me?"

Go on then, tell her. Tell her what you want from her.

"Nothing."

"Bullshit. Everyone wants something."

"I don't. At least not that I'm aware of."

Now *there's* a distinction. Maybe that's worth exploring. Awareness. Do you think?

Is something there, if you're unaware?

"Will," Mr. Jacks interrupts. "Will, it appears that one of your . . . things . . . has gone missing. You know anything about that? You know you're not supposed to remove any of the works." Unless they are specially commissioned for his mother.

"I know, Mr. Jacks. That I'm not supposed to remove them. So I don't know. What happened."

"Hmm," Jacks says, and walks away.

"You stole one of your own . . . things," Angela says with an incredulous half grin.

"Could I come watch you again today?" you ask her.

She was shaking her head before you'd even asked. "No."

"Oh. Okay. I see. Okay."

"There is no practice today."

You have not been rejected, Will. Congratulations. You may as well proceed.

"Would you like to come play bocce with me?"

"Play *what*? I mean, the answer is no, but, play *what*?"

"Nevermind." You're talking into your shirt. What did you expect, after all? "Italian lawn bowling. Nevermind."

Angela's face is now all contorted. "Ya, that's a good idea, neverminding. Let's nevermind, huh?"

She goes back to work. You stare at your gnome with the face that nobody can see but you. You pick up your mallet, and your chisel, and you stare and you stare more, as if you are going to make it take shape with nothing sharper than your glares and the laser zigzags of your mind.

Then you slam down the tools and walk over to Angela's workspace.

"It's just that, I figure, you don't have any friends around here like I don't have any friends around here, and so maybe, we could just, y'know. I don't know."

"Whoa. Time out. The reason *I* don't have any friends around here is that people suck and I'm not interested. The reason *you* don't have any friends is that you're a damn weirdo. The main reason I talked to you in the first place was that I figured being seen with you would make me even scarier and less approachable."

She is joking with you, Will. Half, anyway. Don't you think she's half joking with you? That would be a good sign, actually, right?

If she were joking. Maybe. Maybe not.

"Oh. I see."

You all but bow before taking your leave, returning to your spot, gathering up your tools, and embedding that chisel a good three inches in, right between the gnome's eyes.

She is standing right in front of you. Both of you. Neither you nor the gnome appears to notice, but that is not true, is it? You know she's there. You both know she's there.

"Listen, this is all wrong. It got kind of confused. *You're* kind of confused. I came to this place to run. That's it. Track and field and minding my own business and if they want me to assemble shelving to earn my spot then fine. I said hi to you once, fine, it was like a freak solidarity thing maybe. I didn't mean for it to be a relationship. That was my mistake."

You figure that's an apology?

"Are you a freak?" you ask. Hopefully.

Finally you do look at her. And find her very much looking at you. It's a punishing look.

"No, my mistake again. I am not interested in talking about myself."

"But you said that's why—"

"What is *your* story, creepy boy? That's the real

question. You been here three months already, and you still got this mystery shit all over you."

"I don't have a story."

"Oh, now I *know* you got a story, and it's probably a hummer. You gonna tell it to me?"

You gonna?

You gonna?

You gonna?

What else is there? Where else is there to go?

You gonna tell your story?

Do.

"No," you say.

She is about to leave. "Good. I was afraid you were gonna tell me."

She is about to leave. Will. Do you want her to leave? Do you want that? What do you want, Will?

"I don't know what I want with you," you announce. And that is all.

A kind of a growl thing comes out of her. You are trying her patience. But it is not the unfriendliest growl you have ever heard.

"Okay, there's this vigil sort of a deal. Down at the pond. For that girl who died. That's where I'm going this afternoon."

Angela pauses. Under the mistaken impression that you will be able to take the logical step into the breach and say something. You know better though.

"So do you want to go?" she asks finally.

"Yes," you say.

"Did you know her?"

Did you know her?

"No," you say.

There is a pond, sitting in the bottom of a grassy glacial bowl that sits next to a smaller, drier grassy glacial bowl just outside of town. As if two glaciers stopped by for a sit twenty thousand years back, had a look around, then got up and went on their way again. More recently this location is renowned as someplace you come to have picnics or beer or sex. It is equally famous for what you do not have here. A swim.

Everybody knows this. It is not a safe swimming hole. No one even claims to know how deep it is, with its forest of underwater vines thriving so thick under there that the Loch Ness Monster could still hide successfully even if the water all dried up.

This is not legend, this is fact. Fact enough that even though it can be a very inviting sleepy-looking little pool, nobody takes the great obvious dare.

Nobody who doesn't want to be dead, anyway.

You are sitting on one of the slopes rising steadily away from the wilting willow tree that is growing as it has for ages, half in and half out of the water. It looks, as it has likewise looked for ages, as if it is ready to quit this life and tumble in.

Right now, though, it is hosting the most lifelike event

it has seen in quite some time—the unhappy hoopla surrounding the unfortunate and untimely death of a seventeen-year-old girl.

"Can you believe this has happened?" Angela asks. She is asking you, probably, since you are the only person within the sound of her voice, but other than that she does not seem to be communicating with you personally.

"I can believe it," you say. "Why wouldn't you believe it? It's right there."

Right there is actually about sixty yards away but it is deadly unmistakable all the same. A carpet of flowers, yellows and pinks and whites and reds, fans out from the base of the tree and covers the same area as the shade cover that same willow would throw at the high point of a sunny summer day. Also you can make out other, non-flower things, tributes, difficult to see clearly but familiar enough at dead spots these days. Little hand-printed signs of undying affection, and teddy bears.

And there is one more thing. Like the centerpiece of the whole affair. Leaning gracefully against the tree. It's got a certain power to it somehow, and good thing too, since these high schoolers gathered here would really have no experience in conducting this kind of thing, and in fact there is a danger of the entire proceeding dissipating without some kind of focal point.

And they all seem to have caught it. Nice work there. Fitting. Somebody knows his business. This sad black business.

"So what *is* your story?" Angela asks.

You get to your feet. *"What?"* you ask nervously. "Why should I have a story? Is this about me?"

Is this about you? Will? What's your story? Tell us a story.

She is staring, and leaning away from you. "Maybe. What are you jumping for?"

"It's about *her*." You are pointing, down there, down at the shrine, and down at *her*, even though she's not actually down there.

Why should we believe you? You don't appear to believe yourself. Do you believe yourself? What's your story?

"Is it, though?" she asks. "I mean, I don't know. Why do people come to these things? I'm not sure why I did even. But if you know, I'm listening."

She doesn't believe you know. She is looking you up and down and up and down, you planted rigid like a totem stuck here in the side of the hill, symbolizing god knows what.

You are visible, conspicuous. You are aware. Suddenly, almost involuntarily, you drop to the ground. "Can we just maybe sit here quietly for a while and, like, watch? That would be the *respectful* thing to do, wouldn't it? We owe her that, I think."

You owe her. You owe. When are you paid up?

Angela continues to sit calmly. She shakes her head. "I don't *owe* anybody anything."

You stare down for a second, trying to work it out. Is she testing? Is she for real? Is this a conversation? Triple-thinking yourself again, coming full circle back to nowhere. You clutch two tufts of grassy turf. Tether, Will. Hold on, and try not to give all away.

For a tenuous silent minute or so, the two of you manage to watch uneventfully. It is mad cacophonous noisy on the inside. You have no idea what the outside shows.

"So," Angela says, "did you kill somebody or something?"

You remain silent. You clutch harder at the grass. If this is what shows . . .

"Sorry," she says.

You manage after that to stay quiet long enough to think more and more about the girl. She was a fixture around town. Pretty but not gorgeous. Popular but not wildly so. Social to the point of being somebody you thought you saw almost everywhere, but who you probably saw less than that. Neither here nor there, but everywhere. That's why you knew her, because everyone around here did. You didn't stare, abnormally, you looked, like anybody would. Just because you didn't speak, didn't mean you didn't know.

"Did she kill herself, you think?" Angela asks, extra quiet. As though there is some harm in the question itself.

You slide, on the seat of your pants, a few feet down the hill, toward the thinning gathering, away from Angela.

She catches up.

You slide farther.

It now looks like some sort of an inchworm race, the two of you scooting your way down the hill, digging in your heels, dragging your bodies along behind.

Angela isn't long patient with this. With you. Watch it, boy. You might lose this. You don't want to lose this, do you? Or does it matter? Does anything matter?

"Right," she says sternly, from three feet behind you. "You want company, you don't want company. You want to talk, you don't want to talk. I never asked to have you dogging me, you know, and I can get along just fine without this, you understand? So don't *bother* with all the moody broody, all right, because I do not care."

Did you hear that? Did you hear it, Will?

"Did you even hear me?"

With your back to her, you are well protected, aren't you? She cannot see you biting your lip, can she? She cannot see the way your face is now folded into that singular arrangement of conflicting lines that amount to something closer to a fractured mirror image than one coherent expression. She can't see it. Oh, do let her see it. Because you know she's not going to make the effort to peer around. She doesn't care, remember? People don't.

"Damn," she says as she brushes past on her way downhill. "What do you think we're here for, *you*?"

There's a question. You want to field this one, before she's too far off? Are we here for you? Is everyone here for you? Is everyone everywhere here for you? Or against you?

You watch her pound down the green hillside and whether you are here for you or for the dead girl or the dead girl's family or the six o'clock newscam or whoever, right now you cannot think past Angela. She is a force. All athlete, all tall and sinew and control. She is a mountain goat, same speed uphill or down or sideways, apparently never taking a misstep, or a cautious one.

You get to your feet. Cautiously, you go after her.

By the time you get there, to the tree, a lot of folks have left. The ones who are there are mostly paired off in couples or huddled in threes to stare blankly red-eyed, or to sob quietly and hold one another. Angela, though, has gone dead front center, getting right to the heart of the matter.

"Do you suppose it matters, is all I was thinking," you say, telling her not *all* you were thinking, but certainly a part of what you were thinking. You have come up close behind her, unusual for you. Unprecedented for you. She allows it, as you speak closely enough to her small copper-brown ear. "I mean, whether she did that to herself or not. Does it really matter, to what life is about?"

"When did you do that?" Angela asks, pointing ahead at your carefully sculpted wooden contribution to the tribute. It is a fine piece of wood. You didn't ruin it.

You are both facing the same way, looking at the same thing, faces inches apart. Frozen in tableau.

"I don't know," you say.

"Cut the shit now," Angela says, pulling away from

you and turning to look at your face. "Are you suggesting that somebody else took one of your sculptures out of the school and planted it here? Is that it?"

You run through the possibilities. There aren't many, actually.

"I'm . . . I'm having a hard time . . ." is the closest you can come.

She turns again, to it, then again, to you. "So you started it all. That must have been here before everything else. Because it all seems to sort of grow, out of your thing there. You're the architect of this."

You shake your head, wave a hand. "No. I'm no . . . of anything."

She looks ready to tear into you. But why? What did you do? Do you know? Does she? Was it bad, was it good?

It sure would be nice if Angela would tell you, so you'd know.

"What happened to you, before you came here?" she asks gently.

You close your mouth as tight as you can, making those rigid white muscle lines grow like tentacles from your lips. You close your eyes just as tight.

That is your move, isn't it, Will? From when you were a kid. Still expecting that it is you who disappears when you shut your eyes. That the world spins around *you*.

You open them again. She is still there. You are still there. You are lucky. Do you know that? Do you feel it?

"How do you suppose they figure it out?" you ask.

"Whether it was suicide or not? I mean, can they ever know for sure? I don't think they can. You cannot ever ever know really what is in there, even if you are right there with somebody. So no way can you know after they take the whole secret with them and go. Don't you think?"

"Will. I won't tell anybody. Hell, you're the only person in the school I've talked to in a month."

"I came here to live with my grandparents."

"That wasn't the question. It's a start though, I suppose."

"I suppose."

"And why?"

Yes, why? Will? Hello?

"Hello? Will? You don't want to talk about it. That's cool. I shouldn't do this. You don't want to talk about it, fine."

But you do. Don't you? And you're blowing it. Talk. Go on and talk. Tell her, everything you know. Tell. Her. Everything.

"I was going to be a pilot," you say. Your eyes are suddenly so watery you could be looking at her from the bottom of a chlorine pool. "But they put me in shop. Wood shop. Tied me up in wood shop. The opposite of learning to be a pilot. Like a punishment."

Now you have done it. Don't you ever tire of it? Don't you ever wonder what it would be like to talk to somebody and *not* scare her away?

She goes right up to the sculpture, rubs her hand over

it, and as she does, you can feel it in your own fingertips. The hours of careful rubbing, just so, not too fast, but not too slow, until there is nothing but butter there to the touch. She looks at it and talks to you.

"It is very nice, what you did. It is very nice. Beautiful."

Beautiful. That didn't hurt a bit.

"You know," you say, backing up, backing up the hill, backing away from Angela and the poor lovely girl whom you knew. Did you know her? "Even if you did like guys, I wouldn't bother you. I wouldn't even think of it."

You make her smile. She still has her hand on the piece. She looks your way, smiles a rare broad grin that makes her look about half as old. "I think I know that already," she says.

She does not try to persuade you not to go.

Listen to it, Will. You are the one who keeps setting the alarm to turn on the radio to talk the talk and deliver you the news before your being gets filled with anything as useless as music or the goodness of oatmeal. So you listen.

People are copycats. Teenagers are worst of all. Why be like that, when life is still fairly new and all the choices are still wide-open? What is wrong with people, that they are doomed to repeat what has come before?

Helpless? Is that what they believe? That they are locked into a pattern of behavior that was established perhaps before they were born, and so when they get the signal, they leap?

Small towns are the worst, aren't they? Why is it that one sad sorry story has to lead into another? Shouldn't it, if life made any sense at all, work the other way around? Cautionary tale, and all?

Hear that? This one was seventeen. Say, you are seventeen, aren't you? This one was also a guy, though he was neither a pilot nor a woodworker. And, importantly, *this* sad unfortunate young man dated that sad unfortunate young lady, while you never did. You've never dated anybody, so you're safe there.

This time, you are not alone.

In the murky blue of predawn, she is already there when you arrive at the bridge. The diving point.

The point of departure.

You know how you manage it. You manage it because you keep setting the foolish alarm ever earlier. You should sleep more. Even when you lie there, hour blooming on hour, you know you are not doing anything like sleep.

But Angela. What is she doing here? You were to be first. You are supposed to be first. You like being first. Second isn't even close.

So you should be more upset than this.

"Hi," you say as if you had been expecting her, which makes no sense.

"Hi," she says in the same way, which makes plenty.

You lay the wood carefully against the riveted steel abutment near the hundred-year-old dedication plaque, high above the burbling brown river.

"So then. What are you doing here?"

She shrugs. "Grieving. Mourning. I'm curious. I'm a ghoul. I'm afraid. You tell me."

You nod. Good move there. Could mean a lot of things. Could mean nothing. In your own ways, both speaking exactly the same language.

"You don't seem the type to be afraid," you say.

"That's appearances for ya," she says.

You go to the edge together, peer over together. Talk doesn't come easy now. Talk never does. But this is worse, these things more impossible. You have more experience with this than most, but always you are lost for the right things to say. So you say other things.

"Sure is dirty water," you say. "I don't think I could throw myself into that."

"Because it's dirty," she says flatly.

"Uh-huh."

"I see. So this is what you do for fun."

You move along the rail, away from her.

"What is that move?" she says harshly. "You know, you could just say 'Shut up, Angela. That's not true. You're wrong,' instead of doing that slither-away maneuver."

"You're wrong," you say.

"So slither on back then."

You do. "For fun?" you ask.

"Ya, what do you do for fun?"

"I like bocce ball. And, you know, I do the shopping and other stuff for my grandparents. Stuff like that."

Now she looks like she will be the one slithering away. But she doesn't, yet.

"That's not fun, that's minimum security."

Something comes out of you now. Unusual. Unheard of. It frightens you, doesn't it? Because it doesn't come out of your eyes or your pores or your nose. It comes out of *you*, from somewhere in the diaphram region and sounds as foreign to your ear as Mandarin Chinese.

Is that a laugh?

"Was that a laugh, just come up out of you, or are you gonna be sick?"

You have a hand on your belly. "I think I'm okay," you say.

That must be how skydiving feels. Terrifying but thrilling at the same time. You're thinking about that right now, aren't you, as you look down. Skydiving.

"There's no doubt about this one, huh?" Angela says. "He did it."

"He did. I suppose. There's always doubt. But . . ."

"They still don't know about her, though. Not for sure."

"Never will," you say. "Never can. A person takes that with them, no matter what the cops or anybody think they know. Nobody ever knows who's responsible for anything if they don't see it with their own eyes. Or even if they do see it. Nobody knows anything, that's what I think."

"You don't really think that, do you?"

"Yes I do."

"Come on. I think maybe he did it. That's what I think. Did her, then himself. A guy would do something like that."

You couldn't possibly speak any slower than this. "Cannot know. Nobody can know what happened."

"What if they find a note? That'll tell it, for certain."

You shake your head.

"What do you mean, no?"

"If you are not inside someone's head, or they are not inside yours, then how can you ever know one hundred percent anything about them?"

Sometimes, even if you are in the head. You still can't know. Isn't that so?

The sun is coming up, pale and milky in an unclear morning sky. The water below, looking like Willy Wonka's chocolate river now in daylight, is going past faster than you thought.

"Is this what you've been carving these things for all along?"

"No."

"Then what you been carving 'em for?"

"I don't know."

"Then what you bringing them to these places for?"

"I don't know."

"What do you get out of it?"

"I don't know."

"What do you know, Will?"

"Nothing. Angela, I don't know a thing."

With a sudden, spasmodic shove, you are away from the bridge rail. Standing three feet back, and now looking at the wood carving as if it is a surprise guest at your little party, you say to Angela, "I know this: I need to go finish that stupid fat-face little gnome."

She checks her watch. "Yup," she says, and you start off.

First Angela, then you, as you make your way back over the bridge toward school, pass a hand over the woodwork. Stroking its rounded top, looking down on it. It fits. The way the plaque fits, the railing fits, the abutment fits, as if it were incorporated into the design of the lovely miserable old gray structure. It probably won't even get noticed for the first few hours, as drivers pass it by feeling like it has been there all along forever. No fuss. Good.

You walk in a file, she first, you following.

"Do I scare you at all?" you ask.

"Not at all," she says.

"So you get it, then. Like, you understand."

"Not at all," she says.

What did you think, that you were going to slip one past her? That by tricking her into saying the wrong thing somehow the contract would be legal and binding and therefore you would make sense because you made sense to Angela? Is that what you were hoping to achieve? To cheat your way in?

"So why are you bothering?" you ask, rather recklessly.

"I don't know," she says.

HOPE

YOU HAVE always loved the beach. Always loved waters. Moving waters most of all. Could never resist the pull. Is it the magician's trick, the waving of the cape, coming and going, the possibility of tides and river runs that can produce something out of nowhere or that can take something away just as quick? Is that it then, the idea that what is coming and what is going presents the possibility of something better than what you've got right here right now? That what you cannot see under there has got to be better than that which you can see?

What are you waiting for? Ever believing, aren't you, that a good tide is going to bring you a superior something?

Only now more than ever you like the beach when no one else is there to appreciate it. Which means you like your beaches best cold and windy and rainy and raw and awful.

The severed head of a tuna is a joy.

You look around in every direction, as if a wad of fifty-dollar bills has just blown in your path and you are afraid the owner is going to come flying after it. But no, the tuna head is all yours.

You go close, face-to-face with it. You open your mouth wide, like it does. You touch a very pointy tooth. Your hair is now beaten down hard on your frosted head, by the wind and spray, but it is not uncomfortable. Looking around the back you can see where the spine has been neatly sawed, where the fishermen have removed the useless bits at the dock a half mile to the south. Would have been nice if this find had been the rubbish of a shark's meal. There would be a certain savage kick to that, a primal bloody rightness. But this isn't bad either.

And neither is "Summer Wind," playing in your head, like it does without fail every time you hit this beach. The autumn wind, and the winter wind, have come and gone . . .

Then just like that you are no longer a pair alone. You are a trio. He comes up behind you, the other big skeletal gape-mouthed tuna head.

"Hey nutter," Pops says. "No jacket, no hat, no brains? I'm going to come down here one of these times and find you looking like *him*." He is squatting next to you, pointing at the tuna.

"Ah, it's not so cold."

"And you're scratching again. Quit with the scratching, or you're not going to have any hide at all. You know that's the best way to get some kind of infection, don't you?"

"I do, Pops." Of course you do, but this is what you

do at the beach. It's the salt, probably. The wind, probably. The sand and the salt picked up by that wind and driven by it and embedded into your pores, probably, that make you scratch. It always passes, when you leave the beach. It will pass.

"Skin. Best protector you've got. Take care of it. There's not much we can do to hold back the years, but we can do that." His own looks like the outside of an old suitcase. "And drink that V8, for crying out loud. The supply is all backing up, so I know you've not been drinking it."

"Sorry, Pops," you say. You both know you have no intention of drinking the V8.

For a while the two of you merely crouch there, facing the decaying skull of a creature that was once as big as both of you. Are you waiting for it to speak? You look like you are waiting for it to speak. It probably won't, you know.

"School called," Pops says.

"As they do," you say.

"You need to go, Will."

"I do go."

"Yes, but you need to go all the time."

"Oh. Okay." Like this is news to you. You both also know this is not likely to happen.

"Have you been stealing stuff from the school, Will?"

"No way. Did somebody say that? Who would say that?"

"Fella named Jacks. Shop teacher."

"Those were mine. I made those."

"But they are really school property, yes?"

"Technically. He just wants me to make a stupid gnome for his mother. She can steal them but I can't."

"So just make the stupid gnome. Then go back to what you want to do."

A monster wave builds and builds, and the two of you are pulled, watching the rearing up, the building and cresting and crashing of it. Tide coming in now, and the frothy fingers come touching the tuna just slightly. Won't be long.

"Right, then after that he wants me to make her a whirligig. It's not going to end."

"So speed it up. Make him a gnomeygig."

You smile, but you don't half mean it. It is not lost on you, where you are at, and why you are at it. You know, don't you, Will? And Pops knows, because he is one of the architects.

"I'm not a fucking case, Pops."

"It's not like that."

"Yes it is. I'm in the fucking rehab ward. I'm in with the dead-enders. Everyone there is either stupid or dangerous or hiding out. It's for people who don't *want* to go to normal school. I *want* to go to normal school, Pops. Why did you stick me in there? I don't belong there. I'm supposed to be a pilot."

Now he stands, and backs up. "Tide's coming in fast now," he says, to make like that is what he is backing away from. The wave comes closer this time, coming up all around the jaw of the tuna, giving it a white Abe Lincoln beard, and you wet shoes. "Come back out of there, Will. You are wet enough already."

You get to your feet and take a couple steps back.

"Stop scratching, dammit," Pops says.

You are taxing Pops's patience again, Will. Must you do that? Are you aware you are doing it? Of course you are. You know this is hard for him. You know he is trying. You know what he can and cannot do. He is renowned for what he can and cannot do. Why do you want to make it harder than it already is?

Could it be harder than it already is? For either of you?

"If I'm going to be stuck in occupational therapy, in *special programs*—did you know that, Pops, that they call that *special programs*? Of course you did. But did you know that it's called Hopeless High by the locals? Bet you didn't."

You think? You really think he didn't know? Debatable. Do you want a debate?

"Listen," Pops says carefully, but not quietly. He has to growl somewhat to beat the crash of the surf, but also, he has to growl to beat you. "You agreed. We had an agreement. You were going to try. So. Try."

The *agreement*. Remember the agreement? If Pops was going to *agree* to be stuck with you, then you were going to *agree* to try and get normal? Sure you recall.

"I am trying."

"Not really. You have your father's gift for drama."

Oh. We can ignore that. Do you do yourself any favors if you react? You don't have to. Will, you don't have to. Are you rising to the bait? Your tuna friend rose to the bait. Look at him.

Do you want to fail any more tests? Can you *afford* to fail any more of life's tests, big or small?

Or is it even one? He doesn't do it on purpose. He has no more control of this than you do. Let each other off once in a while. Can you do that?

"Don't start on my dad, Pops."

Let it go. You don't have to.

You are pointing a long, hard, angry finger at your father's father. Is that what you want to do?

"Put that finger down, young man," he says.

What do you think he thinks? Do you think the whole thing is hard for him? Do you think it is harder to lose your father or your son?

Do you think it was your fault?

WillWillWillWillWillWillWillWillWillWillWill.

Do you think it was his fault?

Does one of you owe something?

What do you suppose he thinks?

Do you give a shit?

"I don't give a shit," you say. But you do slowly lower your hand as directed. You turn your back to him now and watch as the tide attempts, in small grabs, to take back the head that it gave you. It looks like a hard job, a big heavy mother job. But in increments, it will get done. The tide will win. It always does.

It is impossible to hear it, but you know your slope-shouldered grandfather is fighting his way back up the beach. He is headed to work in his garden, just as sure as you are sitting there. His garden is your beach. Only when he runs and hides, at least things grow in his wake.

This never works out quite the way you intend it, does it? Probably not the way he intends it either. But he tries. You know that he tries. You give him that, even if you don't tell him.

But there is no book. No rules, no diagrams. Seat-of-the-pants flying, for both of you.

"Sorry, Pops," you scream, toward the sea, as it takes back its gift.

Odds are long that he heard you. But you will assume he did. And if he did he will be waving the wave he waves, without looking back. To acknowledge, and absolve you.

But you don't need to look to see if he's doing it. You slink into a cross-legged lump in the cold wet sand, staring staring at rotting skulls and white horses and gray horizon and vast, vast, vast untold.

Why can't we do better than this? If everyone is to survive we have to do better than this.

So whose turn is it? Who's next? That'll be the question. Do you know? There has to be a next, right? These things always happen in threes, don't they? Don't they always happen in threes? Why is that?

So, who?

Do you know?

You're afraid you might.

"Here it is, Mr. Jacks."

"Will." Mr. Jacks springs up out of his office chair to greet you. He acts as if it is a surprise and an honor to have you arrive, even though you are a student and arriving is the barest minimum of what you are supposed to do. What do they think? Has it sunk to where the barest minimum is more than you can manage?

What are the options after that?

"Oh," he says, taking the gnome out of your hands and examining it like he's some kind of art collector making a very important purchase. "Oh," he says, twisting it around, rubbing it, looking into its eyes ears and nose. "Yes, ah yes, this is good, Will. My mother will be thrilled with it. Very fine work."

It isn't though, is it? It isn't, because you made no effort to make it so. A gnome is a gnome is a gnome, and you some time ago became disconnected from the very freakishness, garishness, inhumanity of the creatures. Do you understand why anyone would want one? The only way you could make any kind of distinctive statement would be to make the thing look human, friendly, pleasant. But you're not capable of that either. So the only distinctive feature of this guy is the morbid thrust of his eyes, bulging two inches out of the sockets. Like when they find drowning victims washed up on your shore, or people who've been hanged. He does, however, have a nice, fat face.

"Great," Mr. Jacks says weakly.

"Thanks, Mr. Jacks," you say, backing out of the office quickly. "I'll just get back to work then."

"Hold on," he says, dropping the gnome onto his desk hard, as he comes to shut the door. "I haven't even given you your next assignment yet."

"Do I really need one? I mean, can't I just go back to doing what I feel like?"

"Well," he says, "I'd really rather see some more of . . . your best stuff. Frankly you seemed to be losing your way for a while there."

Ah.

There it is.

Your way.

Can't be losing that.

Not again.

That's why you are where you are, isn't that it? It's not because somebody might have topped somebody and then did himself. It's not because one day you had parents of a sort and the next day you didn't. That stuff happens to people every single stinking day, and you don't get framed for it.

No, you're here because of you, Will, not because of anybody else. Because you lost your way once.

And how many chances you suppose you get with that? Two? Yes, two sounds about right, doesn't it? We can't let you get lost again. You hear? You hearing? Who are you listening to? We can't let you get lost again. Listen to what you're hearing.

Lost a second time means you don't come back. Do you understand? Lost twice is gone for good.

"Are you listening? Will? Are you listening to me?"

Who are you going to listen to? Who's a boy going to listen to?

"I didn't lose anything, Mr. Jacks. I just wanted to do something besides gnomes and furniture."

Apparently—and surprisingly, considering the population he works with—Mr. Jacks does not have a great gift for handling situations like this, situations like you.

He puts his hand on your shoulder. "We really need you making gnomes and furniture, Will. The world needs something from each of us, and what the world needs from you is gnomes and whirligigs and furniture."

If he had been joking, it would have been very funny, and relaxing. He wasn't, and it wasn't.

You are walking out the door as he tells you, "So no more of those things you were sculpting, okay? And the rest of them, just leave them be. We're not going to make an issue of the ones that have gone missing, but in exchange you don't remove any more school property. Fair enough?"

"Fair enough," you say.

You haven't a clue what that even means, do you? Fair enough. Is anything fair enough? It's like there's this arrangement where we acknowledge that we won't ever have *fair*, so we'll just settle for fair *enough*. And it's never enough, is it?

You walk out into the workshop and it comes to your eye as if it is in neon. It has been there all along, since the beginning of time or at any rate since the beginning of your time in this place but you never quite noticed it before. But you must have. The words have been in there, burned in your head, all along, all during your confinement. The sign that looms—carved capably in wood, of course—above the shop door. You walk under it every time you come into the class and you walk under it every time you go out again and you work almost directly under it when you are working.

BE NOT IDLE.

Well, of course. Isn't that what shop, shops, work-shops are all about? Alternatives to the devil's workshop, right? Busy hands. Flying woodchips for snow, falling over fevered young brow.

Except, what idleness do we mean?

You know what they mean.

"Fair enough," you say out loud. "Fair enough. I won't be idle. Not anymore."

So you go, or anyway, you attempt to go. Marching straight across the room, not stopping at your station, not cleaning up your wood shavings or shelving your important carving implements. You head for the door. You make the door. An achievement right there. You are through the door. You stand there, numbly. Now what? Now what, Will? What was the plan? What is the plan? On what impulse did you propel yourself through that room and out the other side, out into—what? Into nothing and nowhere? Do you think the people inside noticed your demonstration, of strength, clearheaded determination, and be-not-idleness?

Do you suppose you are missed?

Do you care?

You stand for a good full three minutes before turning and staring at the door you so proudly came out from. And you edge it open. Looking inside, looking at all the busy, not-so-busy, and idle beavers in the woody wood center, you notice.

You notice—that nobody notices.

You go back in.

"Come on," you say to Angela.

"Come on, what?"

"Come on with me. Bug out."

"It's a little late for that. You're already bugged out."

"Come on, take a day off with me."

"You are confused. I, unlike you, am here because I want to be here, remember? I have no reason to go."

You wait on that. How many times does she have to remind you that you are confused?

"I'm asking you to go. That's a reason."

Angela stops gluing two bits of a spice rack together to look up at you. "You remain confused," she says. Then she goes back to work. "Why don't you just go back to work?"

How do you feel, Will? Go on now. You feel something. This is . . . your friend, right?

Right?

Or are you confused? Maybe we should pause. Have you got a friend here, Will? Or anywhere?

Why isn't she up on her feet and traveling with you to a better place? Why isn't she being not idle with you, rather than remaining locked in this mine chipping away at nothing, like everybody else? She knows better. Don't you think she knows better? Isn't that why you picked her out? Or did she pick you? Even more so then, if she picked you, she knows. She is different. What do you feel, Will? What do you feel?

Anything?

If it's not friendship . . .

She told you, Will. Why don't you listen? You should listen.

She's a ghoul. Likes deadness. And you are dripping in it.

So maybe then, if you are causing death, attracting death, being death, you are of interest. And if you are a common confused young man who just can't make his way . . . then don't be wasting people's time.

You listening for once? When are you going to listen?

"Okay," you say softly. "Okay, I'll just go by myself. See ya."

"See ya," she answers, just as airily.

Once again you are out there, out in the nowhere corridor with no one. Well, *you* are there, aren't you, so you are not quite with no one. Never alone if you are with yourself, isn't that right? And in the end,

                    and the beginning,

                           and all the days in between,

isn't that really what it is anyway? That you are with yourself, alone. People are nearby, in front of your face or working shoulder to shoulder or whatever it is, but they are never ever really *with* you, are they? Nearby, that's the best they can ever be. Not their fault. Nobody's fault. Just the impossibility of it, is all.

But still you stand there, outside that door, and nobody else does. There are a good many bodies inside the room, but none where you are. No matter. You wouldn't even be talking to any of them, but for the odd obligatory, are-you-using-that-planer-right-now type of shop exchange. They would just be bodies, near your body.

You stare ahead, away from the shop, toward the entire rest of the world beyond the shop. Where and what? Will? Where and what and why?

And then, you are back, through the door, to your station, on your stool. You have a block of soft pine in one hand. Turning it, turning it, before picking up a carving tool once you can see in there the shape of a blade of a whirligig.

There is, of course, another large and teary and entirely well-meaning demonstration of love and support for teenage casualty number two. There are flowers. There are teddy bears. There are balloons and notes and teenagers with, for a change, authentic reasons for stumbling across the brown river bridge looking dazed and confused.

And there is your monument to the meaning of it all.

Which is?

Will?

"Will?" Gran asks through the closed door of your room. She is very good, Gran, about respecting your privacy, your *space* as she so earnestly calls it. She respects your space in much the same way most people do these days, which is about the same way people respect the space of an electrified fence.

"Are you all right?" she asks in the warm and woolly tone between fondness and fear.

"I am, Gran, thanks."

You give her as much reassurance as you can by raising the pitch of your voice without raising your head from the pillow and without offering the extra sentence or two that might actually relieve her concern. You know the scene, Will. You know the signs and the tip-offs as well as she does and you know why she is hovering and you could just as easily defuse the thing as let it burn on. You know these things now, just as everybody seems to know them now, just as nobody seemed to know them back before when the information might have done some good. You could make it better, if only a little better, but still you don't. Why not? Why don't you want it better?

"Do you want something to eat? I could fix you something to eat."

"No, thank you, Gran. I'm fine."

Like there. You could just let her do the fixing, as you know well how happy she is in the kitchen especially working on remedial nutrition for a bone rack like you. Busy hands. Being not idle, don't you know. Or did you think that applied only to you? Did you think that, Will? That the whole show is a show? All the people around you, the grandparents and teachers and *helping professionals* and wood shop flotsam all set up for the purpose of sustaining the almost-life that is you? Did you ever consider that being not idle might apply to people who aren't even you? Doesn't mean you would have to actually eat the food.

"Gran?" you say.

"Yes?"

Do you hear that, Will? Do you hear the hope in her voice? Do you hear the power of the word, of your word, as she waits and wants and wishes to somehow be able to deliver? Go ahead, if you still won't believe, run it again. Go on and roll a second time, ask, and listen to hear if Gran's lips brush the door panel because she is leaning so hard into you.

"Gran?"

"Yes?"

Yes.

"Do you think I could bring the small TV up here into my room?"

And you can hear that too, can't you? You can hear quite clearly as that little bit of something whooshes out of her, like a puff of steam, when you ask for that next extra bit of isolation.

She wants to say no. You know she wants to say no. No would be good, helpful, right. See how it can all hinge on the smallest thing? You could have said, Sure, Gran, I'd love a sandwich, and who knows? She could, should now say, No, it would be unhealthy for you to lock yourself away with the television up here. You'd almost like her to say that, wouldn't you?

Wouldn't it be nice to hear *no*, at the right time?

"I suppose," she says wearily. "I suppose, for a while anyway."

Why? Why can't we do what we know we need to do?

How do you suppose things would be different, if we could change one small thing in the sequence?

But the sequence continues, unchallenged, eh, Will? Can you not change it? Can we change sequences?

Do not look away this time, boy. Not this time.

"Thanks, Gran."

• • •

Can you take somebody with you, do you think? When you go down *there* where you go, where you are now going. Do you have that kind of power, that your descent can pull someone else along?

Conspicuous in his silence since you have taken to your bed—isn't that quaint, the way you can make that sound, *taken to your bed*—is Pops. Pops isn't here. He's there. Here and there may mean only the physical distance of the twenty-foot length of hallway between the two bedrooms, but here and there can be entire worlds apart, can't they?

You have barely been aware of his presence through this, though Gran makes her infrequent kind fumbling attempts to coax you out into the light. You hear him, leaving the bathroom as you are about to use it yourself. You hurry, you make deliberate noise, he speeds up, and closes his bedroom door just as you open yours. You hover outside his door, to hear what you can hear. He could very well be holding his breath.

He will not be coming into your world, if this is what you choose to make of it. Know this. He won't come near. He cannot. He is afraid, and will allow you to go there rather than risk reaching out and being pulled all the way under.

The bed is comfortable, the food robotically delivered by your grandmother is life-sustaining, even if you only consume the merest niblets of each dish of *pasta alla olia* with white beans or bowl of Tuscany tomato soup. You do not move around very much and therefore don't sweat and therefore don't need to shower as regularly as usual.

And anyway why would you need to go to the world when the world comes to you out of the box. Game shows and talk shows and soaps and game shows and talk shows. But that is all filler, in between news broadcasts. Broadcasts which cannot seem to avoid presenting the airbrushing of two otherwise unremarkable young folks as if it mattered.

Still investigating, the beautiful-haired television man says, the connection between the two deaths. What is not in question, however, is the magnificence of the tribute. Even tamped down into that small pixilated TV picture, that bridge scene is one breathtaking monument to young life that will stay young.

"Will?" It is your Gran. "Will?" she calls again. "You have company." It is an effort for Gran not to sound giddy at this announcement, and she only partly manages it.

"No I don't," you say because the thought is simply too ludicrous to contemplate.

"Well . . . yes, I believe you do," she says.

"No, I don't think—"

"Hope you're decent," Angela says, "because I'm coming in there."

Panic. Why? Didn't you want to be missed? Weren't you hoping that somebody would miss you if you removed yourself? Isn't that, in fact, what people like you are up to?

That's right, people like you. Don't dare think there are none.

"So can I come in?"

"Can she? Can she come in, Will?" Gran adds with such unbridled hope in her voice that she somehow manages to make you appear even more pathetic than you are.

"Yes," you sigh. You prop up in bed, rigid as a corpse at an old Irish wake. You make a dismal attempt at presentability, buttoning the top button of your N.Y. Yankees pajamas and smoothing your hair, which by now has become as moldable as Play-Doh.

All wasted effort anyway. Angela sweeps into the room and your Gran sweeps away from it just as conspicuously. Before you have even had the chance to apologize for the state of the place and the self, she is seated on the side of the bed, practically in contact with your blanketed hip, as casually as if you were working in shop. She doesn't care a lick what you look like. Which is a good thing.

"So," she says. "Having a little vacation, are you?"

"I guess," you say. "Why are you here?"

"Jacks asked me to."

"You? He did?"

Angela shrugs. "I'm the only person ever witnessed talking to you, so I suppose I was a natural choice."

"Natural enough, I suppose." You don't like it, do you, Will? The clinical sound of it. You almost expect her to produce some Department of Social Services paperwork for you to sign, attesting to your still-alivability, so she can be on her way. So. What did you expect then? You make yourself a non-person flyspeck of a creature of no consequence, and then what? Long to be of consequence? You wanted maybe for her to come in on bended knee, begging you to rejoin the race? You wanted her to bring flowers from the class and balloons from Jacks and a teddy bear from the headmaster and a great big gigantic card signed by everyone you don't know wishing you a speedy recovery and return? Well, unfortunately, you are a victim of your own success. You don't hardly exist.

"Okay, it wasn't *only* that Jacks asked me to do it. I also, maybe, felt a little responsible. Like, you know, the last time I saw you you were asking me to bag out of school with you and I said no. So I thought maybe you were, I don't know, killing yourself over that."

That may have been a joke. You have no idea.

"And you wouldn't want to miss *that*," you say flatly.

You look at her and she looks back. Refusing to respond. Refusing to acknowledge. Or to deny.

Fair enough.

You look at the TV, in that way that tells a person, without pointing or speaking, that you want them to look at what you are looking at. She does not need to be told twice.

"Ya, and there's that," she says sadly.

Then you both just watch. It lasts about a minute. Long by local news standards. This is big news in a small town.

"Sculpture looks nice, though," she says. "Everybody says so."

Everybody says so. Everybody is saying.

You look and look until the image goes away and an infomercial for revolutionary cookware replaces it.

You start nodding, nodding, agreeing with something, long before you begin speaking. She is watching you getting more sure of the agreement, nodding harder and quicker.

"You want me to go?" Angela asks.

You continue nodding.

"My dad drove off the road," you say.

This is the first time you have yet caught Angela at all off guard. "Oh," she says. She starts to say more, but says the same again. "Oh."

"Into the water. With my stepmother." You continue to nod, as if you are not *telling* the story but are instead listening to it, and agreeing with it.

"Oh. I'm, you know, sorry. Was this . . . do you mean, like, recently?"

You nod. "'Bout a year ago. He adored Sinatra. Sinatra died right after. The truth is I think my dad was some kind of *carrier pigeon* of death. The real surprise is that people around him actually lived, not that they died. Or maybe not surprise, maybe accident is a better word. Or mistake, even, is a better word."

Angela looks sad. You had not achieved that before. How does that feel? Did you want that? Careless. It is easy to be careless, no?

"But he did love Sinatra, though. Loved him nuts."

He certainly did.

"I'm sorry to hear."

"You don't like Sinatra?"

"No . . . sorry to hear, about the accident."

"Wasn't any accident."

You do not know that. That is not knowable.

"'Scuse?"

"There was no good reason for them to have gone off the road. They could find no good reason for the crash. He just killed them both. They were only married a year, just like he was with my real mother before she died. Maybe there was, like, a time limit . . ." You shrug. Your great lying cowardly shrug.

What would they know, investigators, about *good reasons*? What would they know? What would *you* know?

"He thought he could fly, was the thing. He used to say that. That he could fly, but he just didn't know how. He was trying, I figure. He wasn't trying to hurt anybody. He was just trying to fly. I figure."

He did say that, didn't he? You remember that. You remember?

"Oh," Angela says. Could be worse. She could be tripping over herself and saying "sorry" all over the place the way people do. Oh is okay. At least it doesn't sound like pity, does it? Listen close, Will, because it matters. Does it sound like pity, coming out of this one?

"So that's why you're crazy then?" she says casually.

71

Not pity. Isn't that a relief?

"Yes," you allow. "I suppose that is why."

She nods. "You're one up on most of us. Least you *know* your reason."

She looks all around your room. Even you are aware of the stagnant quality of the air and the weird way everything regardless of its actual hue seems to look yellow. What is she thinking? Can you imagine?

"So, you really want to stay in here?" she asks.

You shake your head.

Before she proceeds any further, she gets a bit of a worry flickering across her face. "Listen," Angela says, and wouldn't you swear if you closed your eyes that she was speaking to more than one person? "Don't go misunderstanding. I don't want you thinking that we're going to wind up going to proms together and shit, because that's not going to happen. Right?"

"Right."

"I just figure a soul that's destitute enough to attend track practices is a soul that could use a hand up. Right?"

"Right."

This is reasonable enough. Angela is quite clear on the subject of not having much use for people. You are quite clearly not much of a person. Match made in heaven.

You get up, look about the room for clothes.

"Um," she says politely, "you will be showering, I assume."

You look down at yourself, as if that will tell you anything.

"I wasn't planning to."

She shakes her head. "Whatever. Just don't be getting too close to me. You're kind of ripe."

You wander the room, collecting bits of clothing from various surfaces, gathering them up in your arms in an aromatic lump that even you have to admit bears a strong resemblance to the laundry pile. You stop, stare.

"What?" Angela asks.

"You really think I'm crazy?"

She stares back. And stares back. You may not know a great deal about this girl but you know that she is not one to shy from a question. She stares some more. Looks like she wants to say something. Then looks like she wants not to. After a bit, you both give up waiting.

How does that feel, Will? How does it feel? Are people so afraid of what will happen that they will not risk misspeaking to you?

"If you can wait ten minutes . . . I'll be out in ten. You won't go anywhere."

"I won't go anywhere," she says, graciously turning her attention to the important matters of television rather than your monumental decision to bathe.

It's been three days. Has it been three days? It seems that it couldn't have been. That would be too long, that would be crazy. But when the hot water strikes the virgin surface of your skin from face to throat to chest like thousands of poison needles, you know it has been some time, much time, too much time.

You love showers. You love showers even when you do not need them. How could it have been three days?

You soap yourself quickly, gently, slathering copious amounts of the liquid shower gel all over. When there is no unfoamed patch of skin left visible, you raise the bottle high and douse yourself, like a locker-room scene after a World Series victory.

Cleansing. Now don't you feel foolish? How could you not have wanted this? Foolish, foolish. Clean is good. Clean is very very good. You love that feeling. Make a note, William, to remember that you love that feeling of clean even when getting into the shower seems like too much work.

Toweling off. How many joys had you forgotten in three days? Even toweling off, the shedding of that new soapy skin, like a snake, shedding the old one only to emerge with more vibrant colors that were hidden underneath. Madly, you buff up the head, getting the hair to stand at attention to let the air coolly slide through, bracing the scalp, skull, possibly the brain. The stuff. That is the stuff. The stuff you forget, but that you must not, must not, must not forget, if you are going to make it. Promise not to forget, Will.

So much of the nonsense of you has run down the drain by the time you have left the bathroom you are fairly bouncing as you push open your bedroom door. You are in the early stages of a laugh, aren't you? Of a laugh at yourself, or at least that rancid self that would not groom himself. You are ready, to talk to Angela, to blow it all away, the foolishness that was so inconsequential that all it took was for Angela to walk in and tell you you stink for the world to spin right once again.

Only she is not there to tell. Why is she not there to tell? What are you thinking, Will? Are you thinking you scared her off? Are you thinking that she just got you into the shower in order to make her escape once she saw what a lost cause you actually were?

Maybe you disappointed her by surviving.

Are you thinking that she was right to go? Are you thinking that she was wrong to go? Are you thinking this just proves everything? That it is all preordained? That it is a matter of time? That you are beyond reach, and that even if you were not nobody really can be bothered to do the reaching? You are nobody's responsibility in the end after all, isn't that right? As nobody is really anybody's responsibility.

You are calm on the outside. You are standing there in your clean khakis and T-shirt, staring down at your jumbled N.Y. Yankees pajamas on the bed. You pick up the top, put it on, button it all the way up.

Downstairs, you hear voices, and you follow.

At the kitchen table are Angela, Gran, and Pops. The women are sipping tea. The man is breathing into the knuckles of his folded hands. All conversation stops as you walk in. Gran's face is laminated as she lowers her cup, with smeary tears and runny nose. Pops's face is a granite sculpture, dignified lifeless rendering of one of those great Greek philosophers who knew everything but never really existed.

"Hi," Angela finally says.

"Hi," you say. "Listen, I'm going to pass for today. I'm feeling really tired again. I figure by probably tomorrow I'll be feeling more up to it. So, thanks anyway. Thanks for coming. Sorry to disappoint." You turn and start walking out of the kitchen, walking back to sanctuary or its opposite up there in your room.

Until you feel the small tug at the tail of your N.Y. Yankees pajama top. You turn around to face her.

"Nice getup," she says. "You look like a total tourist."

You put up no resistance. That can be a good thing, if you are not-fighting for the right reason. But you don't need to be told that. You know. You know all about this stuff. Possibly, you know too much about it.

The two of you are headed out the door, with the hopeful silence of your grandparents at your back.

What's it like? It's like this. It is like you are not walking but swimming, out the front door of the house. Like you are being taught to scuba dive, this is your first trip down with the instructor, Angela is the instructor, and Gran and Pops are big silent fish floating behind. They are obviously afraid of making the wrong move, the wrong sound, which would catch your attention and alter your behavior and history. Making them responsible.

So they float, as the entire world at this moment appears to float. You are led along by Angela, by the hand, and as unnatural as it seems, it is not an entirely unpleasant sensation.

Bloop. Nothing but the odd air-bubble noise at your back as you wade out into the world that is three days older than the last time you saw it.

Hasn't changed much, has it? Has it?

"So what am I, like an experiment, a curiosity, a vigil?" you ask as the two of you walk along toward the actual water. Water that even people who aren't crazy can see.

Are you ever walking along toward anything but water?

She looks at you blankly. You are fairly resistant to learning, are you not? Could you not have guessed by now that this is not the way to talk to this person?

"So, what are you up for today? Some wild grocery shopping maybe?"

"Not up for anything. I'm out here because you brought me out."

"Makes me kind of responsible for whatever you do now, huh?"

There's a thought. You could live with that thought probably. Somebody finally being responsible for your behavior. It's the answer, isn't it, to the question you have been aching to ask, if you had the nerve.

Who's responsible?

"Sure," you say. "You want the job?"

"I do not, thank you very much."

"Then why did you—"

"You know, a sense of humor wouldn't do you any harm. From what I can tell, you are completely without one. Are you aware of that?"

Well?

"No. Actually, no, I am not aware of that."

This is where the conversation pauses because, after all, where is it supposed to go from there? You are too old, Will, to develop a character trait as large as a sense of humor now, don't you think? Where would you get one? How would you go about cultivating it? She is right, it is missing, and having it would be a blessing. But you were not wired that way. You were not blessed. And somebody owes you an apology for that.

But you must press on without. Perhaps what you do not have is made up by those around you who do?

"Knock knock," you say.

"Oh my god," she says.

Please don't.

"Knock knock," you say.

"I am *not* answering that door," she says.

"Knock knock," you say.

"Who's there?" she says as ponderously as if she had a bowling ball riveted to her chin.

"You," you say.

"Oh my god, I can't believe you want me to say yoo-hoo. It's even worse than I thought," she says.

Another large merciful silence ensues and when you

emerge you are standing in front of the spot on the bridge which you have been watching on the television. Many many flowers lie there, browning in the May sun, crippled Mylar balloons struggle to beat the inevitable pull of the pavement, melted-down stump candles cling to the ground. There are a couple fresher bunches of blooms still hanging to bits of dirt from somebody's front yard, but for the most part, this service is over. Your sculpture, however, remains, stately and unchanged. First to arrive at the party, last to leave.

"Whatever happened to the first one of these?" Angela asks. "The one from, you know, the other spot?"

You haven't even considered that, have you? Would your work simply return to mother earth when it no longer served a purpose, like the carnations and bluebells?

"I don't know," you say.

You stare. She stares. You have always been a gifted starer. Great concentration. Unaffected by the goings-on about you.

"You are gifted," Angela says. She goes up to the sculpture, traces lines, shapes, curls, and cuts with her finger.

"No, I'm not actually."

"This isn't ordinary work. I've never seen anything like it."

"It's a mistake. It's nothing. I'm supposed to be a pilot. I don't, honestly, know what I'm doing."

"Right," she says, backing away from it. "I forgot. It's a beautiful accident then."

Could this be true, do you suppose? Could there be such a thing? Can accidents be beautiful? Wouldn't you have to know what you were doing, in order to achieve something worthwhile? What do you think, Will? Do you think? What do you think? Is it all stupid blind accident? Is everybody fooling everybody else?

"Summer Wind." Summer wind could not possibly be an accident.

No.

You walk forward and as a habit barely remembered but obviously embedded, you make a little bow, a genuflection, before respectfully removing your contribution to a moment that has come and gone.

"Can we keep walking?" you ask.

"Of course we can," she says.

The surf is crashing so hard you must defer to it. Angela speaks just as a wave has slapped down, and is hissing its retreat.

"I don't know why I don't come here," she says. "This is my kind of place."

You are about to respond but must wait for the next wave.

"Ya," you say, looking out over it all, the silver sand, green water, sky. It is, in some elemental way, yours, isn't it? Could you tell her that? Could you dare, knowing what she already thinks of you? Who could own this? Who could dare? But you do, don't you. "It kind of stinks in the summer though, when people are here all the time and there's nothing you can do about it."

It is the right moment, when the days are long enough to give you light into the early evening but the breezes are brisk enough to blow lighter souls off the beach. One old-timer is walking his arthritic retriever about two hundred yards away but it might as well be two hundred miles, with the sound and the whip of the wind.

The sculpture lies in the sand between you. Like your baby, the two of you are watching over. Like it could make sand angels, if it had any arms.

"People aren't that bad," Angela says, then hears herself, then starts laughing.

"What?" you ask.

"I can't believe what I sound like. Here's the real deal. There was a poet, who I can't remember now but who I used to like when I was in regular school studying, like poetry and stuff that regular school students study. She said something like . . . how was it . . . ?"

Crash, and sizzle. The sea is the perfect soundtrack to this person before you.

". . . oh right . . . I love humanity, it's just *people*, make me want to puke."

Could this be it, your moment, your breakthrough? She is looking for it. She is looking into your uneducated face for recognition.

And there you produce it. The smile. Could mean a

lot of things though, couldn't it? Doesn't mean necessarily that you got the humor.

Angela cannot sustain the patience to wait out this wave. "That," she screams, "is the sorriest excuse for a grin I have ever seen."

There, the smile broadens. But my, the stuff that is so elemental for everybody else . . .

The tide is at its highest. You know this. You know the tides here, the times, the heights, without ever reading the little block buried on page twelve of the paper where they tell you such things. You just know.

"Seriously though, why are you here?"

She looks at you, at the sculpture, at the sky, at the water, at the sculpture, at you.

"Because you brought me here."

"Seriously though . . ."

She stands up. She knows quite well what you mean. Folds her arms and gazes out at the water.

Try to imagine standing there and not gazing at the water. Can you imagine it, Will? Have you the power? To imagine it or to do it? Does anyone? The pull of the water is so strong, can you conceive of anybody, any of us, daring to resist it?

Are we meant to resist, do you suppose?

She is searching for words. The words are all there, why does anyone need to search for them? She is being careful.

You assist. "Morbid curiosity?" you say.

You understand morbid curiosity, do you not? Why do you understand that, Will, when you understand so little of people and life and the way people live life?

"No," she answers too emphatically.

"I don't mind," you say. "I'm curious myself."

"No," she says.

But you cannot believe her, and you cannot get worked up about it either.

Even if she's here for the show. At least she's here.

"You want to help?" you ask, falling to your knees and digging like a dog.

She does. She drops next to you and in a couple of minutes you have a pile of solid wet sand between you and a compact medium-deep hole in front of you.

"So I'm the freak here, is that what you're saying?" she asks.

"Ya," you say evenly. "But I can live with it if you can."

She stares at you, tilts her head quizzically, then smiles cautiously. "Right, so you do have a sense of humor after all."

What sense of humor?

"This is what you want to do with it?" Angela asks, pointing at the hole.

You nod. "Feels right," you say, plunging the base of the sculpture into the sand like the marines on Iwo Jima. Together you and she pack the sand tight all around it, so that even this wind will not tip it. And you know, because you know, that the tide cannot reach it no matter how it tries.

Together the two of you walk back up the beach, and turn to survey. The low sun is at your back, and the wood looks so perfect, so warm in orange light against the ocean backing, it's as if it has grown there, up out of the ground, rather than having been jammed in there by you.

It is right. So little ever truly is.

Angela puts a hand flat on your back.

"So," she says, "see you at the shop tomorrow." It is not at all a question.

"See me at the shop tomorrow." It is not at all a lie, as far as you can tell.

CHARITY

GOOD MORNING.

Listen to it, Will. I think you ought to listen to this one. First, you are doing the quasi-school thing again. You promised.

Second. Well, second you ought to listen, is all.

"Two more. The third and fourth of the town's tragic roster of teenage suicide victims were found last night drowned in the bay. The couple, local high-schoolers, were said to be a popular, sociable pair who had not exhibited signs of the problems normally associated with teenagers in trouble. They were found after a desperate all-night search after they failed to arrive home as expected last evening. Searchers were alerted to the scene by a sort of totem, planted into the sand at the approximate location on the beach where they were thought to have entered the water. Police are investigating whether the couple themselves or someone else had planted the wooden marker."

Rise and shine.

"No," you say. "No, no, no, no."

But that doesn't help anything, does it? What's done is done. It is not your fault.

"No."

That was not what you intended. You cannot allow yourself—

"No!"

Gran rushes into your room, without even knocking. That has never happened before. But she has probably already been up, waiting, for an hour now. Bad enough. Bad enough, the usual reports. Bad enough, the routine day-to-day that she suspects you are not capable of navigating.

But this. Nobody is ready for this. Not on your beach. By your monument.

"It's all right, Will, it's all right," she says, sitting on the side of your bed and trying to get a loving, grandmotherly grip on you.

"How can that be all right?" you demand. You hop off the bed, and point accusingly at the radio. "Gran, how can that be all right? I did that. I did that."

"You did *not*—"

"I fucking well did. I did it."

The phone is ringing. It is barely past 7 A.M. and the phone is ringing. Nobody is answering.

"Do you think . . . do you really think, Will, that you have that kind of control over things? No, you don't believe that."

"How do you explain . . . ?" You are still pointing at

the radio. As if you really do want an explanation for it. As if you honestly believe there can be one.

But you don't. You don't, do you, believe that there can be an explanation? God help you, kid, you haven't been taught much, but haven't you learned at least that things cannot be explained away? When people go they take the whole story with them, remember that? They take it and leave nothing behind.

You grab a pair of jeans. "Please, Gran," you say, indicating she should leave. The phone starts ringing again.

"Are we answering?" Pops calls from his room. Too casual. He is way too casual. This is alarming.

"No," Gran answers.

"Yes," you answer. Now why would you say that? That is the last thing you want.

It's what you get anyway, huh? Most of the time. The last thing you want is what you get.

The ringing continues. They don't go for answering machines here. Nobody calls much. You either get them or you try again if you really want them. So the ringing continues. Then stops. Then resumes.

Gran is politely out in the hallway now, but cautiously not far from the door.

"Answer it," you call as your head pops through the head hole of a long-sleeved cotton T-shirt.

"No," Gran says.

"What?" Pops says.

Everybody seems to be shouting at each other. Why should everybody be shouting at each other? Even the radio guy seems to be getting louder, seems to be repeating himself over and over. Didn't anything else happen last night? Didn't precious expensive baseball players prance around America's ballparks and politicians bravely uphold our Constitution and the Tokyo Stock Exchange exchange things while we slept, or did the whole world stop functioning all night simply to let this monstrosity pass ahead to the front of the line?

"Where are you going?" Gran asks, walking back in. She would never interrupt you dressing so she must have calculated your dressing time. "Maybe you should just stay home today."

"Thanks, Gran. Thanks anyway."

"Hello," Pops barks into the phone. "Yes.

"Will. Will, it's the guy from the school. Jacks."

"Tell him I'll talk to him when I get there."

Pops tells him. Hangs up. It is ringing again practically before the receiver is down.

"What? How did you get this number? How did you get his name?"

"Who is it, Pops?" You want to know. Do you want to know, though?

"Don't concern yourself, Will," Gran says.

"Who have you been talking to?" Pops demands of whoever it is.

"Who is it, Pops?"

"It's a newsguy. You don't want to talk to a newsguy, do you, Will?"

You don't want to talk to a newsguy, Will.

What are you hesitating for?

"Give me the newsguy, Pops." You head to the phone.

"No," Gran is saying. "No, no, Will, what good could come of this? Don't . . ."

Pops is simply shaking his head at you. "Your funeral," he says.

He did not mean that. He did not mean that. Pops is accident-prone, but not cruel. Supremely, supremely careless man, but not cruel.

You and Pops stare at each other. The look on his face may in fact say he is sorry. Don't wait for his lips to say it, though.

"No," you say to the newsguy, "I am not a sculptor. Yes, I made the carving. Yes, I put it there. I don't . . . didn't, know them at all. I did it, though. I am responsible."

He wants to meet you at the beach. You have school. This has nothing to do with you. Mr. Jacks is expecting you. You can't do yourself any good going to the beach. Your grandparents want you to stay right where you are, with them, where they can watch you and take you bowling and shopping and buy you an Italian ice and keep a good close eye on you and not let this one get away. A favor to them, if you can't bring yourself to see it any other constructive way. Can you take care of yourself for the good of somebody else?

Good question that, Will. What do you suppose is the answer? Can one person take care of himself for the good of another if he can't manage to do it for himself?

"Ya, I'll be there," you say to the newsguy and hang up.

When you turn to face your Gran, who could not be closer if she had accidentally gotten under your shirt when you pulled it on, she looks already lost. Dead, defeated, gone.

"I really wanted you to stay," she says, trembly.

You pat her on the shoulder. What kind of move is that? It's not your move. It's not any real person's move.

"I'll see you later," you say, and slip away. Pops is already nowhere to be found.

What are you going to say? It is best to know what you are going to say to someone. Especially one of these. Don't kid yourself. This is no friend. Of all the things you can do for yourself at this point, not kidding yourself is about the wisest and most helpful.

You have made it this far, Will. There is no reason you can't make it all the way. What do you want to say to this man? And why?

It's not too late, you know. Go on and ask, why?

As the newsguy approaches, you are taking it all in. The Scene. Used to be The Beach. Now it is covered with cops with coffee and gadgets, pretty men and women fighting mightily with their hair before allowing the cameras to roll on odes to young life washed away. A few bouquets of flowers have already made their way here— somebody else in town is getting good at this—but they are blowing away just as quickly. This scene is not about to lie still like the others. The beach doesn't want this. The beach is going to throw it all back, scatter it every which way.

"You are Will." He holds out his hand.

"I am." You hold out yours. "You're the newsguy."

"I have a name," he says.

"Is that important?" you ask, and somehow manage not to be impolite.

"Not at all," newsguy answers.

You walk. Newsguy wants to hang around the spectacle, but you have had enough of it for the moment, so you begin to walk the beach. The remaining two miles of silver sand are even more deserted than usual, because of the excitement at the one spot. So in a way, you get what you want.

Don't forget to get what you want. Don't forget to know what you want. What does newsguy want, Will? He is not your friend. He is not your friend. He is not your friend.

He catches up to you. Brings a small recorder close to your mouth.

"I don't think I could talk to that," you say.

This does not seem to be a shock to him. He produces pen and notebook.

"I did that," you say, before the man can even begin to pick you apart. "I am responsible."

"How, Will?" he asks while walking and scribbling notes at the same time. How can they do that, writing one thing and saying something entirely different? Don't they need to concentrate on one thing or the other? What kind of mind can do that?

"How was it you were responsible? Were you here? Were you with the two of them? How many others were here? What went on?"

He is in an awful hurry, is he not?

"Who told you about me?" you ask calmly.

"Is that important?" he asks.

You are in charge, Will. You are the show. You can make him tell you. You can do whatever you want. You are utterly, thoroughly, gloriously, in charge.

For this one, slight, sick small moment. Then it will be gone. You will not be in charge when it is gone.

"Not at all," you say.

"Great. So tell me how you were involved."

"I don't know."

"Excuse me?"

"I just planted it. And the next morning they were dead."

"Come on, kid, the rumors are already flying around about this cult shit and you might as well tell your story straight, to me, before it gets all morphed into something worse. Let me do you a favor."

A favor.

He is not your friend. He is not your friend. He is not your friend. Listen.

"What are you talking about? Cult? What are you talking about? You are making no sense to me." You are panicking now. He can see this. See what it does to him, Will? What do you see in there? Charity? Is that what you see? Is this the man who will do you a favor? Is it out of the goodness of his heart that he is with you now? Does he want to help you? Who does? Does anybody? Does anybody, help anybody?

"Don't play simple with me now. Kids keep dying, right, and your Nazi goth penis weird whatever shit sculpture keeps showing up at the scene, like, really soon thereafter. Until this time when, it appears, it showed up *before*. What's going on?"

Is this what you expected, Will? Is this what you came for? What in hell *did* you come for?

He is not who you wanted to talk to. You wanted to talk. But not to him.

He is not your friend. Who is your friend?

"Do yourself a favor, kid. Talk to me. Let me give it a spin before the cops give you one."

You have not noticed your acceleration until you see newsguy trying to keep up. Now he is thinking the current thought, writing the previous thought, and running at the same time. In the sand.

"What does the sculpture mean? Where does the

design come from? Are those snakes carved into it?"

You run.

"What are you saying? Are you claiming to be some kind of mystic monster? You know who is going to die, and when, and you go there to mark the occasion?"

"Don't *say* that!" you holler. "Don't be saying that!"

You run.

"Is there a connection between this and your father's murder of your stepmother and his own suicide?"

You stop. You about-face.

He stops, but then comes on again. He is walking toward you, as if to make his point of having caught you.

"Listen," he says with the low-tide waves hissing in the distance. "I understand, see. I know, right, that you can only do what you must. I know that you don't really have a choice in what you're doing." It is the intimacy in his tone, isn't it, Will?

That's the thing, isn't it? Does anything in this long bloodless fucking show feel less trustworthy, than intimacy?

"What is it, Will? Is it a voice? Do you hear voices?"

You need no voice to tell you what you want at this moment.

You throw everything—sadness and rage and the past and abject unspeakable loneliness—behind the hand as you throw it.

The force of it knocks newsguy down backward with you lurching forward on top of him.

"So, you a killer too? Family business?" newsguy says with his hand over his mouth.

This is the first person you have ever hit, but you know right off that the feeling in your hand is a broken bone. It screeches with pain up your arm as you push up off the beach.

You are walking away when the newsguy says, "Do you suppose nobody ever tried to punch me off a story before? Didn't even hurt, anyway. Good luck, freak. You'll need it."

If luck existed, one would have to say you were in need of it. As it does not, it will do you no good to think about it. You have done nothing wrong. That is what you need to think about.

You have done nothing wrong. There is no reason to feel as if you had. That feeling is in there, isn't it, Will?

As it has been for a long time.

It shouldn't be. Getting it out is all that matters now. All that matters. Are you listening? This is what you should be listening to. The only voice you should be listening to. Listen to this voice, Will. The one that owes you the truth. The one that will not go away until it is achieved.

They must be so relieved. What must they have been thinking you were going to do?

At any rate, the grandparents are so happy to have you back, so soon after probably thinking they had lost you forever, that they do the best possible thing. They leave you alone. Pretend you do not even exist. When you walk through the door. When you bumble around the kitchen. When you prowl your way up the stairs, into the room, out of the clothes and into the bed. Naked, but for the bedcovers over your torso and a bag of frozen mixed summer vegetables—peas and tiny cubed carrots and strips of bright red peppers—resting on your throbbing hand, which rests on your humming chest.

And they leave you alone through an unbroken day and night of what may be sleep, may be semi-sleep, but is neither rest nor consciousness.

What do you think? It's out. It's out and out there and in the public domain. It is spoken aloud and acknowledged. What do you think?

How does it feel? Is the job done? Did you kill it, him, us? Is it gone, Will? Is it better? Is it worse? Is it finished, or is it just beginning?

Who did you hit? What did you hit? Did it hurt? Who did it hurt?

It hurts. Doesn't it hurt, Will?

"It hurts. Jesus Christ it hurts."

Good. Good, that you are listening. You don't want to be alone. Must not let yourself get all alone.

"I am all alone."

Of course you're not. Like it or not.

You get up, and the frozen vegetables slide to the floor. You had forgotten. How does the hand feel? It throbs, doesn't it, even through the numbness? It won't just pass.

You can't will it away or ignore it away. In there it stays, broken, blood seeping into the places it's not supposed to go, your body fighting, fighting itself.

How does it feel, Will?

"It hurts."

You pick up the bag, slap it back onto the back of your hand, and you pace the room.

Of course it hurts. How does it *feel*?

"I didn't do anything to anybody. Did I?"

You didn't.

"Did I?"

You didn't.

"*Did* I?"

How does it feel?

"I didn't do anything. I never did anything. Un*fair*. That's how it feels."

Don't fuck yourself waiting for fair. Understand? Listening? You will fuck yourself waiting for fair.

They are out there, at the door. She is, anyway. Pops is probably out gardening in the dark. She is afraid to speak. She is afraid to go away. Afraid to engage, afraid to leave you alone.

You walk to the door, padding not-quite-silently across the carpet in your bare feet, then pressing your entire naked self against the door. She is right there, on the other side of the panel. You can hear her breathing. Can she hear you? Will she speak? Will she risk?

Then there is no breathing. She is gone again, and

you remain, feeling, feeling for the impression of Gran's warmth in the door. You think you can make it out, the Gran-shaped etching of heat in the door. You lean, pressing harder into it, harder as it seeps away, harder.

You are not alone, still.

"I am."

Round and round it goes, pacing the room, sitting on the bed, lying on the bed, marching again.

You catch a half-length vision of yourself in the dresser mirror. Look at you.

Skinny. Naked. Creased.

Killer. Mystic monster. Cult icon.

Panic.

Don't. Will. Don't.

Panic. You retreat, from the mirror, from the image with the fifty ribs ready to launch like arrows straight out of the torso. You back up until you fall on the bed, then scramble, still backward, until you are sitting on the pillow, back flat against the headboard.

You didn't think you could get away with it, is what you are thinking. It always was just a matter of time, and changing schools, cities, and caretakers was never going to alter the way things would go one little bit.

You have been waiting since the day.

You always knew. Now everyone will. You're getting famous.

You wait, sitting up in bed. Nothing to do but wait.

• • •

Nothing looks any different from when you closed your eyes, not the closed door, not the murky stillness of the air, not the classic morbidity of your rigid upright pose. Only now your hand is covered in wet and warm, unfrozen mixed summer vegetables.

The alarm goes off, bang on seven as usual. Not usual, however, is the quick bang of you turning it off again.

Nothing happened, no one came. What were you expecting? Do you even recall?

You are going to school, is that right? Are you going to school? Was it like a particularly nasty storm, upturning some trees, shattering the odd window, but essentially come and gone and now, having weathered it, you will get on with things? Look at the hand.

You are refusing to look at the hand. You do your dressing—back into yesterday's clothes which hadn't gotten much wear after all—mostly with the one hand. Look at the other hand, Will.

Having satisfied yourself that you can function without it, you allow a brief glance. It is enlarged and distorted, fatter now at the outside edge of the hand than anywhere else. The valleys between knuckles have been landfilled to reach the same smooth height as the peaks. There is no sign of a vein or a sinew anywhere on the back of that right hand. And though you cannot see it, you are intensely aware that the continuous line of skeleton beginning at the tip of the pinky finger, running down the hand, through the interchange at the wrist, up the arm, the shoulder, the neck and points everywhere beyond, is broken. As if a part of you is now abandoned and isolated from the whole.

You head for the door, open it with your left hand, and head downstairs.

Where you find a sort of party in your honor.

"Hello," Gran says in a voice so nakedly panic-ridden that if you were not worried before you certainly should be now.

But you are not. You are not worried today. You are not anything today. There is something there that was not there yesterday, and you have to do something about it, Will. There is a distance, a wall, a separation, something dividing you from you, and it cannot be allowed to stand. Listen. Listen. Listen.

"Hello," you say, and take your seat in front of your oatmeal. Without fanfare you address the two men across the table—one of them your ashen-faced grandfather, the other a total, gray-suited stranger—and place your lovely cold glass of freshly squeezed orange juice on the back of your hand.

"Morning, Will," the man says.

"Morning, detective," you say.

What? Did they think you were the only one in the entire game who would be surprised by the police at this point? Exactly how far gone are you supposed to be?

And exactly how far gone are you? Will you answer?

Do you know? You cannot let go, Will. Keep thinking, keep feeling, keep asking and answering us.

"Did you call this one, Pops?"

"I didn't call anybody. And what do you mean, *this one?*"

"Somebody must have called"—you look at today's paper prominently displayed, open to page three—"*him.*"

"I didn't call him, he called here."

"Well why would he call here?"

"He traced you to the school, after the second sculpture appeared at the bridge. He was already working on you before this last one. Will, my name is Lieutenant Dahl."

"Hey," you say.

"That hand looks bad. Want to tell me how you got it?"

Gran sets a cup of tea down in front of Dahl.

"Gran, he's going to take me away, and you're serving him tea?"

"I am not here to take you anywhere, Will. It's just, there's a lot of stuff in there, and I need to look into it. You want to read?" He nudges the paper toward you, even though it is still facing his way, upside down to you. That is as it will stay.

"No thanks."

"It's every bit of it nothing but sick lies anyway," Gran says. Pops says nothing. Pops appears for all the world to be waiting just like the good lieutenant, like every other concerned uninvolved tabloid reader, for the story to unfold. What is your grandfather actually thinking, you might ask. Well don't. You cut him loose from this point, son. Don't count on him, don't work on him, don't try to figure him out or bring him on board. That is complete dead-weight action. Believe it, cut anchor, move on.

"I'm sure it is, ma'am," Dahl says. "I just have to check."

"Check," you say, as if the game is chess, rather than your life.

"Okay. Were you there when those kids went in the water?"

"No."

"So how did you happen to know to start a memorial so soon after?"

"I didn't. I planted it before."

"Before. So, are you claiming then to know about suicides before they happen? Are you claiming, like the newspaper says, to be gifted? Some kind of teenage prophet of death?"

Gran begins sobbing behind you. Pops stares down under the table, at his feet or something.

And you, Will? How do you feel, hearing that?

"Why is the phone not ringing?" you ask seriously. "I would figure the phone would be ringing mental by now. But it's not ringing at all."

"Phone's unplugged. I asked, Will, if you are claiming—"

"I'm not claiming anything."

"Do you know who is next? Do you have any information, about any upcoming—"

"The boy said he doesn't know any shit like that," Pops growls.

You don't. You don't know any such thing. How could you know any such thing? The people who go go, and they take it all with them. You know that much, but that much everybody knows. Other than that, you have no information, right, Will? You do not know who is going to die.

"I am responsible," you say.

"No," Gran gasps.

"Talk to me," Dahl says.

"I just did."

"What did you do, to make yourself responsible?"

"Nothing. I didn't do anything to make myself." You shrug. And even shrugging brings pain to your hand. "I just am. I don't have to do anything, and I'm not the *prophet* of anything. I'm just more like, the carrier pigeon of death."

You start looking around the room. What are you looking for, Will? It isn't there. You look back at Dahl to find that he is now looking around the room. But he seems surer of what he is looking for.

"You should really get Will to a hospital, folks. He should really . . . be looked at. That hand's probably causing him a lot of pain." His focus suddenly, penetratingly, pulls in to you. He is looking well into your eyes, though you are barely looking back. "You're in a great deal of pain, aren't you, Will?"

You look at your hand, then slowly back at Dahl. "Yes. Yes, sir, I am."

"Okay," Dahl says, standing, putting on his hat. "I'm sorry to have troubled you all. I don't think I'll be needing anything else."

There is nothing but silence in the room. Uncommon silence, the kind you cannot create merely by being silent. It is too much.

"Don't you see," you say to the officer, "what it's become? It's that now, kids are, like, *coming* to my sculpture . . ."

He holds up a hand, maybe something left over from his traffic cop days back in a helpful uncomplicated part of his career when he used to be able to help people.

"I know. You don't need to be thinking about this stuff. Go with your grandparents and get fixed up. And take a few days off. Get yourself a nice rest."

And, he wants to tell you, this'll all blow over. He wants to tell you that.

Don't you think it is fairly decent of him not to tell you that? Points for this guy.

"Thank you," you say as both of your grandparents bundle him off and you tuck left-handed into hot cereal gone cold and the morning paper.

A lot of doctors for one hand bone. A lot of interviews to be giving, considering until yesterday you had gone an entire life without giving a single one.

The X ray didn't show a broken bone. That's because the X ray barely showed *any* bone. Too much swelling. You know anyway.

Splint, instead of cast. Take it off when you need to. Not a bad deal. One splint to hold you together.

One splint, and a whole lot of medicine.

And what was with the priest, do you suppose? Will? Suppose they're expecting you to *die* from this? That's what they bring in the priests for, isn't it? Or is it the other thing? A confession?

Does either one bring absolution? Think you should ask? Think you should offer?

Bless me, father, for I am death.

You don't want to take the pills. You don't. For a while anyway, you don't. But without them, there are problems. Pain, is a problem. Related sleeplessness, is another problem. You endure.

You don't have to, you know. You don't have to endure any more pain. You don't have to take the pills. You know this, don't you? You know this, that the choices are all yours, and that there is no predestined anything to stop you, or to start you, doing anything that does not suit you.

What suits *you*?

You don't want to take the pills, and it is good that you don't want to take the pills. It is admirable that you do not want to take pills.

But do you want to be admired? Or do you want the pain to stop? And the sound. You could use the peace. Couldn't you use the peace, Will? Wouldn't you like this to stop, even for just a while?

"Yes, I would like it to stop," you say. Finally, finally, finally. You say.

No shame. There is no shame. You take your pills. You take your peace.

Are you still sleeping? You are seeing, that much is certain.

Certainty. It is the opposite of faith, isn't it? Which would you rather have now?

Reach out your good hand. Try and touch. Tables and shelves and gnomes and whirligigs of all description. A phantasmic, freakish familiar gallery of your own unintentions.

"I was supposed to be a pilot. This all never should have happened."

You are awake, for certain. And you are going to school today. All advice is that you stay exactly where you are, but you will not be taking that advice. Though you will compromise by taking your medications.

And anyway, you are not going to school per se. You are going to *the* school, but not to school. This is not a situation you are condemned to live with, just as nothing in this life will be.

Nothing has to be, Will. It is up to you.

So you are not going to school to work in wood. You

are going to tie up loose ends. You are going to finish unfinished business. You are going to clean out your locker.

You are not an inmate of Special Programs.

You are not a woodworker.

You are a pilot.

You promise your teary grandmother and steely grandfather that you will be at bocce ball in the afternoon. She is always teary grandmother these days, isn't she, and he is always steely grandfather.

"Promise," she says.

"I promise," you say.

"No, *promise*," she says.

"Yes, *promise*," you say. And wonder why it is you have to repeat everything.

You are no sooner in the door—and not the little door into the little isolated freezer case of the woodworking gulag, but the big door into the healthy free-range world of the general Socratic population—than Mr. Jacks is right up there in your face, glad-handing and oversmiling you back to lifelike civilization.

"Great to see you back so soon, Will," Mr. Jacks says, putting an arm around your shoulders.

Like you were Charles Lindbergh. Before he misplaced his baby. They taught you stuff like that once. When you were suitable for history.

Or maybe not Lindbergh. Maybe more like the guy

who murdered the baby.

He is squeezing you awfully tight. "I won't try to escape," you say.

He laughs out loud. Mr. Jacks is a decent enough guy, but you have never heard him laugh. Kind of like hearing a cat yodel.

"No, no, no, Will, not at all . . ." He is not only squeezing you, but steering you down the hall. "I'm just really surprised, and pleased, to see you up and around, and back with us."

You can't even manage it, to do the self-preservation thing briefly. To attempt to even look like you are paying hard attention to the man. He is talking, and you are drifting, like a kite.

People look like they are retreating as you pass through the corridors. You see faces—not clearly, but they are there—seemingly forever. Two girls, bumping shoulders, hush-toning as girls do. But they don't seem to pass. They are looking at you—well of course they are—and you are looking at them. You are going your way and they are coming this way, but you don't ever reach, ever pass. You look at Jacks, like for an explanation, then look at the girls, only they are boys.

They are looking at you, though. Make no mistake.

You want to talk to students. You want to talk. You want to shake somebody's hand and say, listen, I am sorry just like you. Sorrier than you, even.

But as you feel yourself pulling ever gently out of Mr.

Jacks's benevolent grip, you feel him tightening up. No matter anyway. Faces are not opening up to you. They are closing, or shrinking or—inasmuch as you can tell as the viscous shield between you thickens—clenching at the sight of you.

The only certainty is that you are noticed.

Why? Why should you matter now? And why should Jacks even be aware of your arrival? Even if he cared, which you must seriously doubt no matter how genial a guy he is, why would he know? You are one problem amid his hundreds of problem chores, and you're not even supposed to be back for another while yet.

Finally, you feel, hear, see, something different.

"Yo, nice work," comes the muffled voice as you are bumped by a passing student. You turn from Jacks to catch just the black coat, dark hair, black hat, swinging side-to-side gait.

You wipe to clear the eye. Jacks swings you back around to him.

"I have been thinking about this a lot, Will, and I don't think you are quite ready . . ."

"Thinking . . . thinking a lot about *me*?"

"Yes, you shouldn't risk . . ."

"When would you have had time to think about me?"

"It is just too soon. You need to be fully . . ."

He's been tipped. Of course he's been tipped. He has been waiting for you. Alerted by one or more of your grandparents who are probably under official orders to let

111

the world know where you are at all times. What do you think about that? You have become so important all of a sudden that everywhere you go, somebody has made a call to tip somebody off. Your every move is under surveillance.

"Am I going to have to wear one of those electronic ankle bracelets now?"

Jacks does it again. The cat yodels. "It's nothing like that, Will, you know that."

You know nothing of the kind. The smallest certainty is impossible at this moment.

It is exactly then that you become aware of the lightness of being you, the physical near-nothingness of it. You are not a body, not a kite, but a massive inflatable parade character, and Jacks's arm feels suddenly like the thing that is keeping you tethered to this earth. He is, in fact, guiding you, as the two of you newly great and good buddies wend your way, on display, through the crowd.

And some crowd. Look at them, Will. As much as you can look at them through the great distance, the blurring, the milky mist. Mist or no, though, it is a sad, scary view, and while you are wondering whether they are scared of you, you have every right to be the one who is afraid.

There is no life in this building. People are here because they have to be here or because where else are they going to go. It is more manageable for everybody to presume they need to be someplace, rather than having to decide all the time what they should be doing, with whom, where and why. That is why the school is at this moment loaded with students who are not going to learn anything, teachers who aren't going to teach anything, and you.

Choice, Will. It can kill you. It is supposed to be what makes living worthwhile. It is what makes not living an option.

They look so sad. Don't they look so sad? Every last person. You have to keep rubbing and rubbing your eyes to get a clear view of a face but you keep doing it and every time you do you are repaid, with a sad, searching face looking hard back into you before turning quickly away.

You reach out, a blind man's move, trying to grab a touch of somebody who seemed to be right there, but then wasn't. You try a second time, reaching for a denim arm that seems *right there*, but then is gone. You squint at a lone small figure with long black hair. She drops her gaze to the floor.

Lock up your children, and avert your eyes. The teen angel of death comes again.

Jacks is, most likely, utterly lost. He takes each of your moves to be some kind of collapse, and gathers you back up into his benign, unwelcome embrace. You ignore him. Continue lurching, leering, attempting contact, mortifying people.

You never noticed them before. You never looked at them before. They never noticed you either.

That is changed. None of them want to touch, but you are all for sure noticing each other now. Because now you share something. You are all scared and lost, and not one of you knows what comes next.

Certainly you weren't expecting this. You let Jacks lead you blindly, but you didn't figure on seeing any crisp white uniforms again so soon.

"Why are we here? We were going to the shop . . ."

"You have to be cleared to come back to class, Will, that's all. Nurse has to just look you over, give you the all's clear. For your own safety. Don't be concerned."

And you are being examined again. Someone, Ms. Appleton, tall pallid unhealthy-looking school nurse, is looking deep into your eyes. As has happened a lot lately. She is asking you questions about yourself. As has happened a lot lately.

"I am in junior year.

"Yes, I am taking medication.

"The hospital didn't find a break. But I know there is one.

"No, I don't believe they are trying to keep something from me.

"I meant to be a pilot, not a woodworker. It was an administrative error."

The next thing you know, you are headed back out the front door with a note in your hand. The halls are now all empty, but just as silent as they were with all the bodies.

"Just a few more days' rest, that's all," Mr. Jacks is saying. "You don't want to come back too soon until you are feeling up to it."

"I wasn't even coming back," you say weakly, looking back over your shoulder into the heart of the school, but walking compliantly out of it. "I was just here to get my stuff."

"Oh." He seems mystified by this, perhaps by your ability to make a decision. "Well. Well, to tell you the truth, Will, I was going to ask you about that."

"About what?"

"Your things. Where are they?"

"My things? Well, I have a jacket and a Montreal Expos hat in my locker. And at my station a couple of small . . ."

"No, your things. Your *stuff*. Your works."

"My works. My woodworks?"

"Yes. I didn't want to say anything until I had a chance to talk to you myself. Didn't want you in any more . . . difficulty . . ."

Nice word, that. Eh, Will? You are in *difficulty*. How does one get in there, you might ask him. And how does one get out?

"Mr. Jacks, how am I in *difficulty*?"

"Where is your work, Will?"

"What do you mean? It's in the storage with everybody else's."

He shakes his head slowly. "I wanted to give you a chance, Will. I know all about your hard times. But it has to stop now. Where are they?"

It is slow in coming. You want to help. You want to help the police and the teacher and everybody walking wounded with the sad long faces who so badly want to have all the life-lost teenagers put back here where they belong and you will quietly slip back out in exchange because as you and everyone else well knows, you never did. Belong.

It is a trade you would gladly make. Trade. Bring them back. You go in their place. That would be as it should be, you are thinking.

Stop. Choice. You do not choose what others do, William, and others do not choose for you. What they did they did. What your father did or didn't do, he did or didn't do. Their choices. Your choices. You are free to go.

You would think so anyway.

Why can't you think so?

"I swear, Mr. Jacks, I haven't seen my stuff, any of it, since . . ."

He knows. He may not have had faith in you before, but the evidence appears plain enough. He knows now, you don't have them.

"Somebody appears to have taken your works, Will. I'm sorry. I thought it was you."

He all but lifts you through the door, out into the most powerful sunshine you have ever felt. He guides you down the cement stairs where you are unfazed at finding your grandfather sitting in the car.

"Somebody stole my work, Pops," you say as Mr. Jacks helps you into the car the way funeral attendants help the frail old widow into the limo.

You are trying to try. Trying to just get better. But again the ringing begins. Gran and Pops have taken to ignoring it, unplugging it for most of the time unless they are expecting calls, or when they have made calls and simply forgotten to unplug afterward. They are old and getting older every minute now. Forgetting is not unusual.

You answer it.

"Who's next?" The young male caller wants to know.

"Excuse me?" You want to know.

"Where should we go, Reaper? We wanna see. We'll go where you tell us."

"Go to hell then," you say.

"For you we will. With you we will. Say the word."

The word is hang up the phone, Will. Stop listening. What are you there for? You do not have to listen—

"Do you really think I know?" you ask the voice.

"Fuckin' right we do. You the one, Man. And we are ready to follow you anywhere."

"Who's we?"

"Check this out," he says. There is a pause as apparently he boosts his probably outrageously expensive stereo to the max, and a phone-version Sinatra belts, "The summer wind came blowin' in from across the sea . . ."

No no no no. We can't have this, Will. Too much

now, too much. You cannot merely accept everything. Do you stand for anything, Will? Will? Does anything mean anything ultimately? Stand up.

Will?

"How did you know? How did you . . . turn it *off*."

Don't talk to him. Run from him.

"I told you. You're famous. You live quiet for a while till time comes then just bust out of no place. Like Jesus. And then we know everything. You are the one. We are your troops. We believe, Man."

You don't deserve this. You think you do? Is that what you are doing, serving penance here? You don't deserve this.

"I deserve this," you say.

"Yes you do, Angel," he says. "You're chosen."

There are three or four similar, cracked male voices suddenly barking solidarity in the background. Then they start chanting along with Sinatra, making "Summer Wind" sound more like one of those brainless marine drill chants than the greatest song by the greatest crooner of all time. Make them stop. Can you make them stop? Do you stand for anything? Make them stop.

"Who are you?" you ask calmly. "Do I know you?"

The voice on the line suddenly sounds different, as if he is holding the receiver back from his mouth. "I am not important. I am nothing."

Why are you subjecting us to this? Will, hang up the phone. Go out and putter in the garden with your grandparents. They always want you to come into the garden with them and you always fight it. Maybe it is a good time to stop fighting it. You will be surprised how much you can bury in the backyard under layers of fertilizer and rich peat moss. They know well. They will teach you. Put down the phone, Will.

"Do you have my stuff?" you ask softly, as if you are making a black-market deal.

"Nice work, Man," he says, all low and slithery. "Nice, nice work."

You shudder from this. Something goes through you.

"What are you doing with it?" you ask.

The caller's voice goes from secretive to proud. "We saved it, Man. We liberated your works, all of 'em. Couldn't let the authorities keep 'em, could we? We all know what the world does with prophets, don't we, Man?"

Don't we. Man.

"Do I know you?" you ask again.

"'Course you do," he laughs. He addresses his friends then. "He wants to know if he knows us. Is the Man a jokester, or what?"

There is lots of laughter and agreement in the background.

You are a jokester, Will. You. Least humorous creature on the planet. Jokester. Prophet.

"You should give me my stuff back," you say. "You don't even know what it is at all."

There is now a long silence. Then there is intense breathing, like this has turned from a fawning fan call to a merely obscene one.

"Fuckin' 'course we do, Man. We know exactly what it is. We're the only ones who do. We're your—"

"Don't say that again, okay. Just . . . I just need my things back, that's all. I'm not feeling so great, all right, so, if you don't mind . . ."

"I do mind. We mind."

"You don't understand . . ."

"We understand. Better than you do. We're not like the others. We're here to do your work. You'll thank us. In the end, you'll thank us, Man. Just tell us who's gonna be the next one."

"No. I won't—"

You are talking to a dial tone.

The clock tweets. Every hour it tweets—or hoots or burbles or twitters—with the song of the white-breasted nuthatch, northern oriole, or whatever North American songbird happens to be the patron winged creature of that hour. You can only hear the clock, not see it. You haven't the slightest idea what hour has been struck. But you know it is the American robin hour. Beautiful song. Sweetness itself.

"I'm going out," you call.

Who are you telling, Will? There is nobody in the house.

"I am," you answer. "I am in this house. But not for long."

You should not go out. You should not go out now. You cannot do yourself any good out there now.

You go to the front door, knowing well that your care-givers, guardians, benefactors and collateral damage victims are way out back in the garden. They are not as spry as they once were. And less so with every passing event. They will never reach you before you are gone.

"See you later," you call.

Probably, they would not have made much of an effort anyway. One of the sorry facts, that. When we give up, we often give up collectively.

Have they given up, do you suppose?

There, but not there. Your spot, as if you have paid for the season skybox seat high above the track, and it is always there available for you no matter how infrequently you attend, just like the important bigwigs at real sporting events. The truth is, there are loads and loads of other seats that are always available as well. Most of them, in fact.

But this one is yours. Because it is so far away from everything. Looking straight ahead, and down, you can survey all that happens, while all that happens cannot see you back. You are too small, too remote. Behind you, over a railing that is really too low to be safe, is a thrilling seventy-five-foot drop to the unpainted blacktop of the parking lot.

Things are hazy for you. You couldn't recognize a familiar face twenty feet ahead of you if it was standing still, nevermind speedy athletes of only passing acquaintance off yonder in the distance. You are all too aware of this. Why are you here?

She is here. You cannot make her out, but you know she is here, and that is enough.

But no, you can see her. Sure you can. She is coming into focus, coming, coming, coming.

She is outrageously, impossibly, beautiful. Her every move—her every *component* of every move, from the backstroke of her left arm while lifting her right leg, to the bobbing of her head and flaring of her nostrils as she lunges for the tape—is majestic. If you could be her, you could be all right. She works properly. She flows. She is right.

And she is the only one you can see clearly. You realize. All the other beautiful speedy beings continue on their cloudy foggy way while Angela pulls tightly into your focus.

And she looks at you. She has won her event, whatever it is she does. And she has turned suddenly to look up into your special skybox to see that you are up there. You are. She is coming your way. Walking across the oval interior of the track, she ignores the shotput, threads the relayers, hops the low rail, mounts the concrete steps.

Sits next to you. She is covered in sweat. Healthy, perfumy, beady sweat, that you love to be next to, that makes you want to drink it. Not at all like that diesel fluid that comes out of your own pores.

"You shouldn't be here," she says.

"I know that," you say. "You think I don't know that?"

"So?" she says, probingly.

"So," you say, neutrally.

"So what do you want from me?"

Altogether too direct. Altogether. This is not something you are prepared for, is it, Will? You have not been prepared for this. Apologies. You should have been prepared. Better. Long ago. But apologies won't help you now. Listen. Think. Listen, think, respond. Act.

"Nothing."

She sighs. Stands. "Fine."

Now Angela is doing what she does. She is doing. She is walking down the stairs, toward the field and pumping hearts and winning and losing and sweat. Away from you.

And you are doing what?

"Would you miss me?" you blurt.

She stops, turns, looks you over.

You know the lookover. People checking your eyes, your posture, your mannerisms, for signs of whether it's okay to be honest with you or careful with you or if they should even get involved. You know this look, but you don't know it from Angela. From Angela, it could as well be she's looking for the spot to hit you.

"Some. But it would fade." She shrugs. She heads back down the steps.

And there you sit. Watching her leave. Satisfied, are you, Will? Is that what you were after?

You jump to your feet, wobble, steady yourself for one last gasp.

"That's not supposed to be the answer," you yell. "You're not supposed to say that."

Now you have done it. You don't know exactly what *it* is, but you have done it. Angela has turned and is taking the broad concrete steps two at a time to get at you.

"You know how it's *supposed* to work, is that it? You don't know a goddamn thing. Miss you? Miss *you*? Possibly, maybe, I don't know because I don't know who the fuck you *are*. But miss *this*?" She makes a grand sweeping gesture from your head to toe like she's trying to make you disappear. Then she punctuates it by poking you hard in the chest with every last word. "Sorry, junior. Sorry, sorry, and sorry."

Is she sorry, do you think? Do you think? Go on and think, Will. Think.

"You're not sorry."

"Ahhh," she yells, right in your face. "Of course I'm not fucking sorry. *You* are the sorry-ass. You want to go swanning all around the place acting all woe is me, and checking to see who's catching your act. And I guess I'm the lucky one, right? I'm the one who gets to watch?"

Had enough, Will? She doesn't understand you. Nobody understands you. Nobody understands anybody, and everybody's an ass. That about covers it, doesn't it, Will?

"What are you staring at?" she demands. "Why don't you say something, defend yourself, tell me I'm wrong, tell me your secret, tell me I'm the stupidest bitch you ever met, tell me you're Jesus and you're doing all this suffering for me? Why don't you tell me *something*, and give us both a chance to feel sorry for you or better about you? Huh?"

Why not? There's a perfectly good question, Will. Why not. She has certainly given you enough choices.

Or too many. Is that it, Will? Too much choice?

Well, it's too much something, because you remain, lifeless, paralyzed, silent. She waits. She can't wait long though. She won't.

"Shut up," she says to your silence. "Life, okay. Life is a gift. Only you can't return it if it don't fit right. You just grow into it.

"Grow up, Will."

She throws you a disrespectful little mock salute as she spins away, toward the track, toward speed and sweat and heavy breathing and elevated heart rate. She is leaving now and you know she won't turn back again.

"Life goes on," she says, like a dare.

Before you even get a chance to debate that, she is back on the track, back in stride, back to magnificent motion, back to winning, back to blur with the rest of the field.

Back at the glacial pond where you sit on the slope, everything has stopped. There is no trace of anything that was there during the heady days after the first girl went under. Outside of in here, there is a spectacular nothingness of quiet. Not even a ripple on the water. Inside, is another story. It is crippling.

At the bridge, the brown water is running hard. There

is an urgency, as it slaps and swerves its dark path under the bridge, under your feet, past you and gone, but still there and coming all the time, all the same. Small yellow-caps lick up off the surface of the water in your direction. It is a noisy water, full of voice.

The beach, your beach, is not what it was before, and it certainly isn't what it was before that. The celebration has been wiped clean. All evidence gone. All manner of tribute gone. You love that about your beach, don't you? That it just won't put up with it. The ocean takes care of its own business, dumps what it wants to on the shore and takes back what it wants. Sand castles, flowers, teddy bears or heads and bodies. The wind and tide decide.

And they do not care about intentions. Not the cop's intentions or the victim's or the crier's or the reporter's.

And not yours.

You're all wiped clean away.

It is not your place anymore.

It is so loud. It was always loud, your beach. But it is screaming in your ears now and the sound does not blend as it once did into the long creamy understanding sigh it used to because it has shattered into its individual ninety million tiny horrible distinct voices.

You would like the screaming to stop, wouldn't you, Will? You would so like it to stop.

"Look what I found."

It is dark when you wind up, through no effort of your

own, at your own doorstep. Angela is sitting there. She's got something of yours with her.

You are speechless. You did not expect to see either of them again. Did you want to?

"Where did you get that?" you ask.

"My front yard," she says coolly.

You approach, reach out, and start stroking the smooth blond wood. You run a finger into and out of every curve and angle, over every finely sanded bit of surface.

"Excuse me," she says. "I don't mean to interrupt, but, what is this, a present? A joke? A fucking death threat?"

"I don't . . . I'm sorry."

"You're sorry. Yes, we have established that you are very sorry indeed. But that doesn't tell me anything."

"I don't know what it's about."

"You had absolutely no part in this . . . *thing* being planted in front of my house?"

"No. None at all, I swear."

She sits there, scowling at you from the steps of your own residence. Then she nods. "I guess I figured that anyway. Still creepy as all hell, Will. And you are the source of it, whether you planted this one or not. I don't like this, and it has to stop. No more of this shit."

"No," you say weakly, almost to the sculpture. "No, this isn't good, is it? We can't have this."

Your eyes, you can feel, are half closed and aching

from the lack of sleep, the relentless tug of the medications, the wind and the mere effort of constantly trying to focus.

"Go to bed," Angela says, lifelessly. She stands and brushes past you.

"I will take care of this. Don't worry," you say. "I am going to end this."

"That's reassuring," she says bitterly, fading away into the darkness.

You pick it up, carry it on your shoulder into the house.

"Where have you been?" Gran says, shaky.

You take a long, lost pause that cannot very well reassure her. Then, you point to the wood. "I was . . . getting back my stuff," you say. "See. It was at Angela's."

She looks at it, at you, then at her own wringing, wringing hands.

"Are you going to bed, Will?" she pleads. "Just tell me you are going to bed now. You look . . . you look bad. You need to sleep."

"You're right, Gran," you say. "I am bad. And I'm going to sleep."

She nods, and stands at the foot of the stairs until you have made it all the way up. Once there, you turn and wave to her. You may as well be waving from the moon. You even feel it, don't you. The first stirrings of weightlessness. Gravity releasing you from its grip. You shift, one foot, to the other, to the other.

Teeter.

Teeter.

Then, in the hallway, you check the phone. It is as you expected. You plug it back in before going into your room and propping up in bed to wait.

Of course you can't make it. You tip over with exhaustion and don't have the strength to get properly into bed at any time during the night. You sleep on top of the covers, on the side of your face, with your arms tucked underneath you.

You are awake for untold minutes or hours before you can even manage to move.

The clock sings the song, on the hour that belongs to the blue jay. He whistles it out, the rising notes, then pulls it all right back again, the same strong song in reverse. You are still drifting on that song when you hear another, the house wren, a funny question of a tune, like it's surprising itself. Two birds. A whole hour. Just like that.

Finally you arrive on the first floor, still in yesterday's clothes.

"I don't want you going out, not just now," Gran is saying, greeting you at the bottom step. "Can you just do that for me? Just this once?"

"Where's Pops?" you ask. It's all feeling so suspicious at the moment. Something is wrong. Plenty is wrong. Why does Gran have her hands on you? Gran does not put her hands on you, like a cop, to keep you from going out. Why this, why now?

You go to the curved parlor window, parting the hazy

cottony curtains to see Pops scurrying around, taking it all down as best he can. When Gran comes over to get you away from the window, you make your break for the door.

"Just go back inside," Pops says, tossing something into his wheelbarrow. "You don't need to worry yourself about this."

This is, of course, entirely yours to worry about. The front lawn of your grandparents' house has been turned into the public museum of your nightmares.

Could you, really, have created all these things? Did you, really, have the time, the inclination, the energy to carve so many garish, ferocious little beings? Gnomes, gargoyles, whirligigs. Thirty, forty of them, grinning, spinning, leaping. Gap-toothed, horned, eyeless. Long Salvador Dalí mustaches. Some cut sharp as crystal figurines. Some appearing to melt.

They look familiar. One or two, maybe, you remember doing, but they all look familiar. Like distant family.

And in the middle of this loosely arranged circular parade of a tribute to you, is the question. Written in block capital, Day-Glo yellow spray paint in Pops's precious nail-clippered lawn.

NEXT?

They want to know.

They want to know what you know, Will. What do you know, Will?

Do you know?

"Maybe I do."

You do not know, Will. You are not responsible. You do not know.

"Maybe I do."

"You do *what*?" Pops barks at you. "Who are you talking to?"

His eyes are bugging, he is so angry. Sounds like he's angry at you, does it not? How screwy is that? How screwy, and how true? Here it comes. You'd better be ready for this. Are you ready for this?

"Nothing," you say. "Nevermind," you say.

"No, I won't nevermind. I want to know who you were talking to." He has an ugly gnome under his arm. They are all ugly gnomes, of course, but this is an ugly gnome among ugly gnomes. You could swear it grunts when it hits the ground.

"Just leave him alone," Gran pleads with Pops.

"Leaving 'em alone doesn't *work*," he growls. He is accusing her of something.

"Neither does browbeating," she says, accusing him.

They appear, right there, simultaneously, to realize something, to remember something, to conclude something. And just like that they go watery, and nobody wants to get worked up anymore.

"Maybe you just want to lie down, Will," Gran says. "Have you taken your medication?"

"Ya," you say.

"Maybe you want to take some more," Pops says, getting back to collecting monsters off the lawn as if collecting red and orange disintegrating leaves.

No, Will, maybe you don't.

"Maybe I do."

"Will!" Gran gasps.

You don't want to take more.

"Maybe I do. Who's going to tell me what I want and don't want to do?"

"Who are you talking to?" Gran sounds scared. Pops hardly takes note. "Who are you talking to?" she repeats.

Who are you listening to? Pops? Are you listening to Pops? To *him*, Will? Don't we know about him? Don't we? Who are you going to listen to when you come to the end? Who will be there?

"Do you think so, Pops?" you ask, hard.

Pops is already back to the job at hand. The job that involves his hands alone. Busy hands. Pops is a good man with busy hands. If there is a task Pops can address with his hands, that job is as good as done.

Be not idle. Pops.

He is scooping up your ugly scary little wooden phantasms like nobody's business. They are disappearing. His lawn, aside from The Question, is coming back to him.

NEXT?

"What?" he asks, as if the whole issue is a million miles gone behind us now. His hands are very busy.

"Do you suppose I should take more meds? Think that's a good idea, Pops?"

Pops stops. His hands, for the moment, are not busy. Idle. Not at all good.

What does he want to say, Will? Before he says it, it is probably worth noting what he *wants* to say. In case he tries to alter it, like they do for your own good. Can you read it there on his face?

A very old face, no? An old, etched face. Older, even, than his many many long sad years. Are you thinking, perhaps, that what he wants to say is, Yes, take the whole bottle once and for all and for god's sake let everybody else off the hook? Do you think?

"Pain's bad, is it?" he asks sadly.

"It is," you assure him. "It's unbearable."

It is as if your words are not words but numbers, factors of some kind, that he has got to work out every time you speak, before he can speak. An equation he's been trying to figure for a long very long time.

"I don't want you to take the pills, son." He is walking toward the toolshed, head down and mumbling as if he is embarrassing himself. Ashamed of what he's said, done. Not said, not done. "It's only pain, son."

Twice now. Pops has used the word *son* on you in two consecutive mumblings.

You don't know, do you? How uneasily that comes to him. Twice. Do you know what this means? Do you want to know?

"I'm not your son," you say, freezing him in the doorway of his beloved shed.

Why did you say that? Did you have to say that?

He drops his head so low that from your vantage

point he looks like the headless, horseless, horseman. He doesn't so much walk the rest of the way into his shed, as dissolve into it.

So? So.

"So nothing," you say. "I can't be responsible."

"Responsible?" Gran asks. Her voice cuts across your face like a biting wind. You're startled.

You turn to her. "Jeez, Gran, you scared me."

Smack. It is likely this is the first time Gran has hit anyone, and it is surely the first time anyone has hit you for real.

"No," she says, and that could be hate in her voice, if you have any ability to recognize hate or love or indifference. "He is not your father. Nobody understands that better than he does. And I am not your mother, or your father. And *you* are not your father. Nobody is him anymore."

Fair enough.

"We are us. We're what's left. We're it."

You look at her, and wait. What are you waiting for, for her to hit you again? You would like that, wouldn't you? Well, she's not going to do it. For her to tell you what to do? For her to tell you what not to do? You shouldn't expect any more of that, either.

So? What?

You follow, on to the shed, where you find your grandfather in among the gardening gear, various silly sun hats, hoses, an electric snow shovel which gets no use anymore because when it snows now they just stay in the house. And several leering, beaming sharp-featured characters offering lollipops or pansies from their pudgy evil little hands. He is surrounded by them.

You can still only see the silhouette of his hunched bony back.

He is, still, damnably hard to talk to. Is he not damnably hard to talk to?

"For chrissake," you shout, "*everybody* is damnably hard to talk to."

He turns around. You're looking in his face now, as he is looking in yours. And what do you know?

Who'd have figured?

He sees something, somebody, somewhere, in your face, here in the little temple where he hides away, with your little freaks and his rakes as congregation.

He is not even going to ask who the hell you are speaking to.

"Yes they are," he says. "Damnably hard. But you have to try, don't you? Isn't that the thing? That you have to try?"

"Do you, Pops? You think? Maybe you don't have to. Maybe, you know, some people are supposed to just not try. Maybe that's why, some people . . . why things just don't work out for some people, because everything's already set up, the rules are laid out, the dominoes are falling down, and everybody has their bit already made up for them. And maybe some people's

135

bit is just to fuck up, and fall down."

He picks up one of those little claw things gardeners use when they are down on their knees tearing up the dirt. He turns it around and around in his hands, as if there are working parts on it that need his attention, oiling, tightening, whatever.

"No," he says firmly.

You shrug, you try and turn away. "I was just saying, maybe some people—"

"No," he repeats, a little stronger. "It's not set up, and it's not dominoes, Will, it's life. Life is life, and it's not anything else." He is gesturing now, with the claw, and at the same time his gaze is drifting, up to you, then over, and beyond you. He looks like a claw-handed professor, lecturing on something grand and important and probably outside your grasp.

"You get one life. And it's yours, and you are in charge. And all right, somewhere along the line there is a moment when you need more. You need intervention. You need a hand up. Every single person has this moment, but it is only a moment and after that your life is your life again.

"Call it charity, Will, call it love, or call it blind bloody luck, but comes a time when somebody needs somebody else to pull his wagon for him. And you know what? Most of the time, life being what life is, that somebody is right there for you."

You are aware, are you not, that you are extracting something from Pops. That you are making Pops be not

Pops. That he is going where he doesn't go, saying what he does not say, approaching something—

"Is this all of them?" you ask.

"What?" He is stunned. He might be angry.

"Them. The *things*, the woodworks. Is this all of them?"

You can see his teeth, bared now as he speaks. "Are you here, Will? Do you understand what I am saying? If somebody doesn't *make* it in life, it's not because that was the *plan* for him all along. It's just that . . ." His voice drops in half, as he struggles to the end of this. "It's just that somebody wasn't there, with the right help, at the right moment. The people left behind have to live with that.

"But they live with it.

"Do you understand me, Will?"

Do you, Will? You will. Understand? Agree? Give a damn? If you listen, you will know something now. What are you listening to?

"Is this all of the carvings that showed up?"

You have done it now. You have finished him. He drops the claw, turns his back to you, and buries himself in the darkness of the back of the shed.

"That is all of them," he says.

You are looking around. As if he could possibly have missed your most famous work if it was here. No. It's not here, Will. It is still out there, Will. It is not an accident. It is still out there.

And you are responsible.

You stand now, staring at your grandfather's back. The two of you motionless, clueless as to what comes next, as the two of you seem to increasingly be.

And then you are released.

The ringing of the phone far off on the second-floor landing, faint but clear, sends a shock of energy through you. You run.

"That was unplugged," Gran calls desperately from the far end of the yard. "Pops . . ."

Walking has been job enough lately, but running now feels effortless. There is no broken hand now, no petrified filthy clothes hanging on lifeless creaking bone rack of a body.

Ring, bastard, ring, bastard.

The bastard will ring, ten, eleven times. You will get there. He will wait.

You nearly break down as you hit the stairs to the second floor. Your left knee buckles and your right hand reaches out to break the fall, and *there* you feel it, shooting up your arm, shoulder, into your eyes to blind you with the pain and remind you.

You answer with your left hand, and all your remaining breath.

"Hello?"

Dead Frank Sinatra is on the line.

You wait. You can't wait through much of it, though. Not this.

But you can't seem to not listen either.

. . . and still the days . . . those lonely days . . . they go on, and on . . .

"I'm going to hang up," you say finally.

"Don't do that," he says. He turns the music off.

The two of you wait. What are the rules for this? You have both been waiting for this, but now, how does it work?

"Angel, you didn't show," he says. "You let us down."

"What?"

"You know what. The freak chick. She's supposed to be dead now. You fucked up."

You were waiting for this phone call. You were longing for this phone call. Now that it's come, you are paralyzed.

"So what's up?" the voice goes on. "You lost your power? Or was that one just a dud? Is that it? You stick me with a dud? Fuckin' shame, you know, 'cause we really wanted to see the freak chick out. She shouldn't be here . . ."

You sink deeper as he goes on, and on. Deeper into his words, into the morass, for which you see, finally, clearly, indisputably, you are responsible.

You are responsible.

Next?

"You know, right? Of course you know. We know you know."

"Hey," you snap into the phone, you snap off his words.

You let him hang for a second more. Now it's time.

"So you want to see who's next."

Something has changed. With the words, the words you did not know you would say, but which sounded familiar and practiced and inevitable to your own ear.

Right. That's how it feels now. So entirely right. Nothing has felt that way in a long, long while.

You hear a short quick blast of anxious breath shoot out of him before he speaks. "Of course I do. Shit yes."

"So you will. I'm going to the beach. Now. Bring it."

He is saying something, but it does not interest you in the least, as you hang up.

The wind seems to be blowing about a thousand miles an hour as you sit there. The sand is packed wet and cold everywhere, and it's drawing any warmth out of you like a needle pulling blood. But you are not interested in being warm. You would be somehow disappointed, cheated, if you were comfortable.

You are far less surprised than he is.

"Whoa," he says, standing over you in his thigh-length black leather jacket and nearly matching cap. He has got the sculpture under his arm. He is staring at your face.

"You don't look so good."

You have no patience for the sound of his voice. You get to your feet.

"And what did you expect death to look like?"

You rip the wood out of his short-fingered hands, and

140

start walking toward the surf. The tide is halfway in.

"Good to have this back," you say, stroking the wood like a precious Angora cat. "I was worried you'd turn it into a video rack."

He laughs nervously from a couple paces back.

"Right," he says. "Listen, like, I gotta know what we're up to. Who is it? What's going down?"

Your turn to laugh. You like the way he sounds. You like the way all the Sinatra cool runs out of him. You like the smallness of him.

"Should we wait, do you think?" you say, casually. "Maybe we should wait, and get some press coverage. Hardly worth doing something if you don't get credit for it."

"Ha," he says. "Right. Well, you got nothing to worry about, right? You're famous already. You're *there*."

You snort. Then you stop, drop the wood, and spread your arms wide as you lean into the wind off the ocean. You inhale deeply, smelling it, smelling all that's in there under the gray-green secret skin of the ocean.

Here's the spot. Fifty yards from the surf.

You point at the spot. "Let's get to work."

He drops to his knees and digs like a mad dog. You start down to help, but he insists, "No. You're the Man."

"I'm the Man," you say, and shake your head. You turn back to the water.

You could nearly cry, couldn't you? Nearly. It is talking to you. It is simultaneously screaming and whispering to you. It is saying all the names, in all the voices, in angry and sad, and lost and helpless tones.

It is saying your name.

And your name suddenly sounds like the saddest word you have ever heard. Your name, coming off the surface of your adored ocean, is making you want to cry with gratitude and apology.

"Done," he says, jumping to his feet.

You turn, and see that it is in fact done, and done well. Deep and firm, the rooting of this monument. But it stands no chance. The tide will not permit it. It doesn't have long here.

"Nice, nice work," you say, and he cannot help smiling.

You grab him roughly, but friendly. You pull him close, facing him out to sea with your arm around the back of his neck. Your lame hand rests on his collarbone.

"Next . . ." you say.

You pull him closer to you, tighter, harder, and you feel him. You feel that he is nothing. He is barely even there. You squeeze tighter and feel that you could just about lift him off his feet and finally pull tight enough to pop his head right off and boot it into the sea. His deadly cool coat flaps behind him. Perhaps he is a kite.

"Death to the freaks," you say.

He squirms in your grip. You turn your face to examine his, right up close. He smiles broadly from within the headlock. Only because he does not know what else to do. He turns just his eyes toward you.

"You want to be famous. Like me."

He just keeps smiling his petrified smile.

You start walking. Walking him along. Walking to the water. You release him from the headlock but retain a firm grasp on his collar. Leading him toward water.

Thirty yards from the water.

"What are you doing?" he asks.

"Doing what I do. You know what I do. And now I'm going to show *you* what I do. You want to see, right? Wanna do what I do? You wanna go where I go, boy?"

Fifteen yards from the water.

"Trying to fuckin' scare me, is that it?"

He still doesn't understand, does he, Will? Does anybody, do you suppose? Is it even possible, in the end, for anybody to understand anybody?

Still, you try and help him understand.

"Why would I want to scare you? Why would I possibly care, whether you are scared, or brave, or happy, or stupid?"

You reach the water. You do not stop.

He pulls away from you. "I'm not going in there, ya crazy shit."

You are in up to your ankles. You turn to look at him once more.

"Good," you say, and your smile, broad, almost painful, shapes and distorts your words. You don't recognize the voice. "Stay out of my fucking water. Run home to Mommy. It's over for me, but it's just beginning for you. Now *you* be famous. Now *you* be responsible. You're gonna *wish* you came with me."

Maybe it's the bared teeth, the electric voice. Maybe it's the angel of death authority of you. But he listens. He runs. Leather coat flapping away, leather cap flipping right off his head. He refuses to come back for it, as he kicks sand up behind him stride after desperate stride. You watch him run a wide arc around your monument. Your own monument now. He falls. He gets up. He falls again. He gets up. He runs and runs and runs. From whatever plague it is you carry.

He is gone. Everyone is gone. The beach is scoured and empty, your carving as lonely as a flag on the moon.

You are once more on your way. You are up to your knees.

The water actually doesn't feel any colder than the air.

You are up to your hips. You are up to your chest.

Your clothes, hugging you tight, don't even feel wet now. You feel protected, like a channel swimmer coated in grease.

You give one last quick glance over your shoulder as you take the first stroke of your weak Australian crawl which will not get you to Australia.

You are not surprised to find the beach behind you empty of emergency rescue teams, or colonies of benevolent lifesaving penguins.

You crawl away. You crawl your pathetic crawl, and things fall away. Your coating of grease falls away, and you get cold. Sounds of seagulls and waves fall away, and you hear wide gaping incomprehensible ocean instead of articulate shore. You slow down. Your arms get stiff, and heavy, and your shoes feel like bricks.

You stop. You go from crawl, to dog paddle, to treading water.

A rest? Will, a rest? Conserving energy for what, after all?

You love the taste of it, though. Seawater.

You tread some more. What do you expect? You expect nothing.

You crawl away.

Nobody is responsible.

You didn't expect it to be this cold. It is awfully, awfully cold.

Life is a gift. If it doesn't fit, you grow into it.

You remember what a great swimmer you are. How did you manage to forget, what a great swimmer you are? You are a great swimmer, Will. Time is not pulling you under, it is building you up. You are swimming harder, less stiffly. You love the ocean, and it loves you back. You might make it to Australia before you tire.

Call it charity, call it love.

You switch to breaststroke. Your breaststroke is even faster than your crawl. You forgot, how clean and smooth and strong your breaststroke is, even with soaking, frozen clothes on. You are cutting through the water like a small power boat.

Life, being what life is. Somebody is usually there.

A sandpiper swoops down over you, dips a wing, banks toward the shore.

You flip over, float on your back to watch him. He tacks this way, then that. He glides briefly, then he beats his wings madly once more. He aims for shore, but in no great rush, with zigs and zags and zigs to spare.

Your backstroke. Oh yes. Your fine, fine backstroke.

You float, staring at the reflective silver ocean sky, and power up the first easy movements of your perfect backstroke.

You forgot.

One thing, one last thing, falls away.

You were not alone. All that time. You were lonely.

At the southeast corner of the world's best-kept garden stands a dogwood tree which will very soon be a screaming pink riot, a suspended rocket-burst of velvet petal which will compliantly turn from bud to canopy to carpet in appreciation of love and attention paid to it. Planted, shallow but firm, at the foot of that tree, is one small monument in wood. Sitting on the ground in front of the monument is an exhausted pair of old gardeners.

At the northwest corner of the world's best-kept garden, just inside the gate, stands the grandson of the exhausted old gardeners, the son of the man they have finally put to rest.

You are wet through to the bones, frozen nearly solid, as you stand looking all around, and see them. As they see you. Poking out of shrubbery, dancing around dusty millers, twirling in the mild breeze or squatting in the far corners of the yard.

You feel a thousand years old, crossing the garden in your wet clothes. You feel as if you're built of rusty wrought iron, crossing the garden. You feel as if you are approaching the finish line of a race you have been running nonstop for a year.

Walking right between your grandparents, you find yourself with two hands resting on the top of a well-turned, beautiful blond piece of wood. It is loud, the sound of your clothes chafing your skin, as you drop to your knees.

"Been someplace?" Pops asks.

"For a swim," you answer.

You read it like Braille. Your fingers lovingly caress the surface, finding each detail so painstakingly laid in for the touch, if not the eye. The initials, the faces, the hands reaching for hands. The breaking waves, the nautilus shells, the shorebirds. The little shadowy somebody. The lonely bare dunes. The summer wind kicking up the tiniest speckles of sand.

You are unaware when she does it, but there she is, your gran, behind you with her hands on your waist, bringing you up off the ground.

"We never really put him to rest, the first time," you say. "We just put him away."

Her little hands squeeze your sides.

You withdraw your hands from the monument, cock your head a bit, regard what you see. "That's a nice piece of work I did there," you say. "It looks good here. I'm pleased."

Pops struggles to his feet, claps you far too hard on the shoulder, which also pleases you. Pops being Pops.

"We need to get you warm, and dry, and fed," Gran says, steering you toward the house like she is pushing the lawn mower.

"Yes we do," you say, and allow yourself to be gently guided through the yard, weaving through the gallery of waving, leering, spinning creatures you created.

Ugly as ever, the tiny bastards. But now, finally, in place.

In their place. In context. Devoid of their spook.